Tom Appleby
Convict Boy

Tom Appleby
Convict Boy

Jackie French

📖 Angus&Robertson
An imprint of HarperCollins*Publishers*

Angus&Robertson
An imprint of HarperCollins*Publishers*, Australia

First published in Australia in 2004
by HarperCollins*Publishers* Pty Limited
ABN 36 009 913 517
A member of the HarperCollinsPublishers (Australia) Pty Limited Group
www.harpercollins.com.au

Text copyright © Jackie French 2004

HarperCollins*Publishers*
25 Ryde Road, Pymble, Sydney, NSW 2073, Australia
31 View Road, Glenfield, Auckland 10, New Zealand
2 Bloor Street East, 20th floor, Toronto, Ontario M4W 1A8, Canada
77–85 Fulham Palace Road, London W6 8JB, United Kingdom
10 East 53rd Street, New York NY 10022, USA

National Library of Australia Cataloguing-in-Publication data:

French, Jackie.
    Tom appleby, convict boy.
    ISBN 0 207 19942 6.
    1. Convicts – Australia – Fiction.
    2. Penal colonies – History – Fiction.
    I. Title.
A823.3

Cover design by Antart. Cover images: top left and bottom, Photolibrary.com;
top right, National Library of Australia.
Typeset in 11/16 Sabon by HarperCollins Design Studio
Printed and bound in Australia by Griffin Press on 60gsm Bulky White

6 5 4 3 2 1   04 05 06 07

To Bryan

chapter one

Murruroo, Australia, 15 April 1868

Thomas Appleby saw the ghost on the morning of his ninetieth birthday.

Thomas rose early, as he always did. When he was young he had been starved of sleep, had longed for a proper bed with sheets. Now his sheets came from Ireland, and smelt of lavender, but his body needed little rest.

Thomas used the chamber pot, then dressed slowly. He was in fine shape for a man his age, as the doctor had told him on his last visit out to Murruroo.

Which means, thought Thomas wryly, that even if my bones ache, I can still hobble down to the river with my walking stick.

Thomas looked out of the window. This, too, was ritual. In the old days he'd checked that all was well — that the 'roos hadn't broken into the corn crop overnight, that a sheep hadn't got cast in wet weather, its wool so heavy it couldn't rise and needed rescuing.

Nowadays he looked out onto lawn and flowers, not sheep or corn. But beyond the river he could still see his paddocks shining autumn gold below the gumtrees.

Some people said that gumtrees looked like old, bent men. But Thomas had always thought they looked like girls with long white limbs, reaching up into the sky.

Thomas blinked. There was someone on the lawn, peering up at the house as though looking for someone.

He peered out of the window again. The figure looked ... strange, somehow. Indistinct. It was almost as though he could see the roses through it, and the green of the grass.

A ghost? Thomas smiled to himself. Ridiculous! Years ago Jem had told him that the ghosts of chimney sweeps haunted the chimneys where they'd died. But Thomas had never seen a ghost — never expected to see one, either.

His eyes must be playing tricks.

Thomas banged on the windowsill with his cane. 'Ahoy, there!' he called.

The ghost — if it was a ghost — paid no attention. It was as though it didn't hear.

For a moment Thomas considered pulling the bell for one of the maids, and ordering her to investigate. But you couldn't ask a maid to hunt for a ghost.

No, he'd go downstairs himself. Thomas grasped his cane firmly and began the journey — for it was a journey now, he admitted to himself, along the hall and down the stairs.

If there was a ghost down there, he'd find it.

chapter two

Puddlington, England, 1785

'Don't look,' said Mistress Palfrey comfortably. 'Poor lambkin, it's not your fault your pa is a blasphemer.'

'He's not,' said Tom tightly, staring across the village square at the mud-splattered face of his father, his head and wrists locked between the thick wooden boards of the stocks. As Tom looked yet another passerby bent down and grabbed a handful of muck from the pond and flung it at the bruised man.

Mistress Palfrey lost some of her smile. 'Well, what do you call it then when a man prints a pamphlet saying His Majesty the King, God save Him, is no better than the rest of us?'

'It was work,' muttered Tom, as the mud dripped from his father's face. 'Pa was paid to print it.'

'Then he should have said no,' said Mistress Palfrey, gathering up her skirts to head back home. She hesitated. 'But you're welcome to a bite tonight, and a bed, too, if you've a mind,' she added over her shoulder. Mistress Palfrey was a kind woman, when she thought to be. 'You can share our Benny's bed.'

Tom nodded, though he had no intention of going to Mistress Palfrey's or sleeping in the same bed as Benny. Benny had been one of the lads who'd pelted Pa with horse droppings that morning.

No — Tom would wait till the village was quiet, then wipe Pa's face again, and bring him water. There was still bread and a bit of bacon in their rooms behind the shop. The mob hadn't taken them when they'd smashed Pa's press and scattered the type, and dragged Pa almost senseless to the magistrate.

It had been the magistrate who'd convicted Pa of blasphemy, and sentenced him to a week in the stocks.

The bread would be hard and stale, but Tom could soak the crusts in water and feed the slops through Pa's swollen lips. Only three days to go now, and Pa would be free.

Tom glanced around. The square was quiet now, the sun high in the sky. Mistress Palfrey and the other women were home cooking dinner, their men at work in the fields. A squirrel ran along the branch above him, peered down, then scampered back up the tree.

I was like that a week ago, thought Tom. I had a safe home to scamper back to. I never thought that things might change as fast as this.

Tom ran across the cobbles to the stocks, sending the pigeons scratching around in the horse droppings into a flutter. With Pa bent over, Tom was almost as tall as he was.

'Pa! Can you hear me? Pa!'

Pa opened one eye. The other was swollen shut. Blood seeped from a cut on his forehead and muck crusted his hair. 'Tom, lad,' he mumbled. 'Shouldn't be here, lad. Shouldn't see this. Go home. Wait there.'

'Soon,' promised Tom. He took his handkerchief, still damp from being dipped in the pond earlier in the morning, and tried to wipe the worst of the dirt from his father's face.

Pa shut his eye. His breathing was harsh and deep.

'I'll be back later,' promised Tom. 'I'll bring more water. Bread, too.'

Pa nodded, though Tom didn't know how much he'd understood. 'Shouldn't be here,' muttered Pa again, and Tom wondered if he meant himself or Tom.

Someone laughed from across the square. It was Benny Palfrey again, with his friends. They had been Tom's friends once. Not now.

'The dog has got his puppy!' called Benny. 'Shall we get him too?' A clod of mud hit Tom in the chest.

Pa's eye opened again, wider than before. 'Go!' he commanded. 'Run, lad. Run!'

A stone hit Tom's neck. It must have been sharp — he felt blood trickle down his skin. Tom ran as another hail of stones began to fall about the stocks.

When he reached the shelter of the oaks he looked back. Pa's head hung down; his hands in the wooden shackles looked loose as well.

Pa had looked like that before. There was no reason for horror to creep across Tom's soul. Yet . . .

'Pa!' he called. 'Pa!'

There was no answer.

Tom ran back across the square. The shower of stones began again, but Tom ignored them. Pa's good eye was open, staring at the ground.

'Pa?' Tom reached up and touched his father's cheek.

Pa didn't move. There was a new cut on his forehead where a rock had knifed the flesh away. It shone red and white amongst the dirt, but didn't bleed.

'Pa!' screamed Tom. Another stone hit his arm. Tom turned in rage. 'Stop!' he screamed.

The boys laughed uneasily. Another rock skidded in the dirt by Tom's feet, then the boys turned away.

'Pa?' whispered Tom. He touched Pa's cheek again. Was it colder already? The sightless eye stared at nothing.

chapter three

1785

It was Mr Tupper the church warden who fetched Tom from the square as dusk was falling. One of the village women had reported that the boy just sat there by the body of his father. Mr Tupper ordered six men to take the body and lay it out for burial, and himself took the boy to the magistrate.

The scent of roast beef lingered in the hall of the great house as the magistrate came out of the dining room, still wiping his chin on his napkin. The candles flickered in their sconces.

'What's this then?'

Mr Tupper touched his forelock. ''Tis the boy Appleby, sir,' he said. 'The father has gone and died in the stocks.'

The magistrate glanced back into the room where his roast beef was cooling. 'Mother?' he barked.

'Died from the typhus, sir, two year ago,' said Mr Tupper. 'The boy be an orphan, right enough.'

'No other family?'

'None that I've heard tell of, sir,' said Mr Tupper.

'Well, boy? What do you say for yourself? Have you family you can go to?'

Tom shook his head. Mr Tupper pinched his ear. 'Speak when you're spoken to,' he hissed.

'No,' said Tom.

Another pinch. 'Say "sir"!' hissed Tupper again.

'No, sir,' said Tom.

The magistrate shrugged indifferently. 'The workhouse, then.' He made to go back to his roast beef, then stopped. He raised an eyebrow at Tom. 'And mind you behave yourself from this time on,' he instructed him. 'Your father came to a bad end. You see that you don't follow him. Do your duty to your God and King and Master.'

Tupper nudged Tom sharply. 'Yes, sir,' said Tom numbly, while inside his mind was screaming: *It was you who killed my father, as much as the boys. You and Mr Tupper, who told the congregation that Pa's pamphlet blasphemed the Lord. You and Mr Tupper and the King.*

The workhouse was in the next town, a two-hour walk or an hour's cart ride away. It was too late to send the boy now. Tupper led Tom down the shadowed drive and up the lane and through the village again.

As they passed the square Tom could see his father's body laid on a wagon, his shirt pulled up to cover his eyes. Tupper caught Tom roughly by the elbow. 'No running off now, my lad.'

'Please,' whispered Tom desperately. 'I want to see my father.'

Tupper ignored him.

Tom slept that night in Tupper's storeroom, smelling of the hams in the ceiling and salt beef in the keg. 'And mind you don't touch neither of them,' ordered Tupper.

Tom nodded, only half hearing him. It had been twelve hours since he'd eaten that morning, and then only the dry bread and a rind of cheese. But his body felt like it had gone beyond food.

The room was dark, but a little moonlight seeped through the high, narrow window, showing the rounded shapes of casks and barrels, the tea chests and the sack of flour. There were more empty sacks, neatly piled behind the door for when they might be needed again for apples or pears.

Tom spread out the thickest sack for a bed, with more rolled up for a pillow and others to pull over him as a blanket, and lay down. The stone floor was cold in spite of the sacks, and hard, but at least there were no mice.

Tom stared at the ceiling, the hams and bacon hanging by their hooks. There was too much for his mind to absorb: his whole past life sliced away from him, the shadows of his future clouding his brain.

If only he could shut his eyes and wake in his own bed, with Pa stoking the fire downstairs, the smell of toast and printer's ink slipping up the stairway.

But Pa was dead.

Tom shut his eyes, then opened them again. The shadowed hams were better than remembering Pa, filthy and helpless. Pa, with the boys mocking him. And unbidden came the thought that Tom had tried so hard to keep away: if only I had stayed with him, Pa would still be alive.

I could have sheltered him with my body, he thought. If I had yelled at the boys earlier, maybe they would have gone away. It's my fault that he is dead. If I'd had courage, Pa would still be alive.

I will never be a coward again, he thought desperately. Everything I had has been taken now. All I have is courage.

Pa had read him a story once, about a knight who wrapped his courage about him like a cloak. Can I do the same? wondered Tom. He tried to imagine courage. It would be a fierce, bold colour — red, perhaps. Yes, courage would be red. A cloak made out of courage would be thick and warm and keep him safe …

Tom slept, or at any rate he shut his eyes and felt the night disappear around him. He was woken by the bolt sliding from the door. It opened and a red face looked in, with a white cap above it.

'Why, it's just a lad,' said a voice. 'Tom Appleby, ain't it?'

Tom sat up on the sacks, blinking. It was Tupper's housekeeper, Mrs Wilson. 'Yes, ma'am,' he said.

Mrs Wilson surveyed him. 'You'd have thought t'master would have given you a bed for the night, with your poor pa not yet in his grave. But there, that's t'master all over, no more thought for others than a goose on the pond. Now you come out of there and have a wash from the tap by the trough. No running off, mind, for it'll do you no good. There'll be breakfast for you when you're done.'

It was a good breakfast: soft bread from that week's baking and fresh butter and cold mutton. Tom's body seemed to take over despite the numbness of his mind. He ate, and ate some more, and was still eating when Tupper yelled from the kitchen passageway for Tom to meet him out the front.

The cart was waiting for him. It was the cart from the hotel, Tupper having none of his own. It smelt of beer barrels and hay.

Tupper looked put upon. He glared at Tom darkly. 'I've more to occupy myself with,' he complained, 'than looking after the likes of you. Make haste now, or it'll be noon before we get there, and the best of the day gone.'

Tom climbed onto the seat beside him as Tupper shook the reins. The old grey horse stepped out into the lane.

Tom had hoped they would go through the village, so he might see Pa again. But the horse turned to the right, not the left.

'Please, sir,' said Tom. He had no wish to 'please' or 'sir' Tupper at all, but knew he'd get no answers unless he did.

'What is it?'

'Will my father have a funeral?'

'He'll be buried like a Christian,' said Tupper. 'Not that he deserves it.'

'May I be there?'

Tupper ignored him, as though the question wasn't worthy of an answer.

Tom watched the oak trees and the last of the cottages pass.

'Sir?' he asked again.

'What is it?'

'My things, back at the shop.'

'Don't you bother about them,' said Tupper. 'They'll have been impounded already.'

Tom had no idea what impounded meant, but he guessed by Tupper's tone that his spare breeches, his neckcloths, the coins in the box below the stairs were lost to him, as was Pa and their years together.

They had taken everything then, the magistrate and the King. His father, his home and his belongings. And slowly there grew a hatred in him, like fire burning in his stomach, against all who had been part of the theft of his life.

The old horse clopped slowly along the lane, unmoved by Tupper's flick of the reins.

'Sir?' Tom spoke quickly before Tupper could order him to be quiet. 'What will happen to me at the workhouse?'

Tupper shrugged. 'You'll be put to work, and good luck to you.'

'As a printer?' asked Tom hopefully. Tom had always

thought he'd follow Pa's trade. Pa had let him set type by himself already.

Tupper gave a bark of laughter. 'Not likely. A factory hand maybe. In the mines, most like.' He gave Tom an assessing glance. 'Not much meat on your bones, though you'd do to pull a coal truck. You'll take what you're given and count yourself lucky. Now be quiet.'

chapter four

The Workhouse, April 1785

The workhouse was a long, two-storey building of grim brick, with bright flowers in beds along its gravelled drive. Tupper drove the cart around the side, then handed the reins to a groom lounging by the stables.

'No need to unharness the horse,' said Tupper to the groom. 'I won't be long.'

Tupper rang the bell at a side door, not the front. The front door, Tom supposed, was for people more important than him or Tupper. A woman opened the door, letting out a smell of cabbage and turpentine. She was tall and her apron was starched white against the black of her dress. She glanced at Tupper, then down at Tom.

'Not another of them!' she sighed. 'What a year. Orphan, I suppose.'

'Father died in the stocks,' said Tupper with ghoulish satisfaction. 'A blasphemer, he was.'

'Terrible. Terrible,' said the starched woman automatically. She stared at Tom again. 'I'll take him from here. Best he goes to the office straightaway, for there's one there who may take him off our hands, God willing, and spare me the trouble of a bed for him.' She nudged Tom. 'Say goodbye and thank you to the good gentleman.'

Tom said nothing. Oxen couldn't have dragged a thankyou from him. He looked at his boots instead. They were good boots, bought new from the cobbler last Christmastide.

'Heathen brat,' said Tupper. 'Like father, like son. We'll be glad to see the back of both of them in the parish, so we will.' He touched his hand to his hat. 'Good day to you, missus.'

'And to you.' The starched woman nudged Tom again. 'That way,' she ordered. 'And mind your manners.'

The corridor was long and narrow. Tom had never known a corridor could be so long before. It opened into another, wider this time, with polished floorboards under a red carpet. Three women in grey overalls scrubbed the far end of it. They didn't look up as Tom and the woman passed.

Finally they came to a polished wooden door. The starched woman opened it without knocking.

'Another boy, sir,' she said.

'What?' The man at the desk looked up. His round face was red and three strands of ginger hair dropped across his shiny pate. 'Well, mayhap we have a lad for you after all,' he said to someone across the room. 'Come in, lad, come in. You may go, Mary,' he added.

'Thank you, sir.' The woman dropped a curtsey and left.

Tom stepped into the room. It smelt of porter, like the front room at the Cock and Hen, and floor polish, and something else as well. Old soot, thought Tom. It smells of soot.

Another man sat in the hard wooden chair across from the desk and its armchair. This man's face was long and very white, and curiously smooth. The only hair that Tom could see was poking out of the man's nose. He wore a shiny black bowler and a leather waistcoat, and his trews were black and shiny, too, from long use.

The soot smell seemed to come from him.

The red-faced man glanced at Tom, assessing him. 'Name?'

'Thomas Appleby, sir.'

'Age?'

'I will be eight next month, sir.'

'Well?' The red-faced man ignored Tom now. 'Will he do?'

The black-and-white man looked at Tom with consideration. 'He be a bit old, like. I like 'em younger. Easier to train. Once they get too big they won't fit up the chimleys.' His voice was high and hoarse.

'He's small enough. And he looks healthy,' urged the red-faced man.

'There is that.' The black-and-white man assessed Tom as if he were a horse he was thinking of buying.

'If you get them too young you risk them dying on you,' said the red-faced man persuasively. 'You lose all the effort you made in training them.'

'There is that, too.' The black-and-white man seemed to come to a decision. 'I'll give ye fifteen shillings for him.'

The red-faced man shook his head. 'Thirty, surely, a well set-up boy like this.'

'Twenty, then.'

'A guinea.'

'Done.' The black-and-white man spat in his palm, then held out his hand to shake on it.

'You've got a bargain,' remarked the red-faced man, smiling so his brown-rimmed teeth showed.

The black-and-white man grinned. 'No more than have ye. No sooner does the lad step into your parlour than ye've sold him off. Yer not even a bread and water dinner poorer. You, lad — what was ye name again?'

'Thomas Appleby,' said Tom, then added, 'sir.'

'Hoity-toity, will you listen to the voice on him? We'll soon knock that out of you,' said the man, his own squeaky voice filled with good humour now at a job well done. 'No room for airs and graces up the chimleys.' He touched his hat to the red-faced man. 'Good day to you, milord.'

Three seconds later they were in the corridor again; a minute later in yet another cart outside. Tom had been in the workhouse for no more than ten minutes.

The cart smelt of soot as well, and soot lingered in its corners. This horse was young, but pitiably thin, its ribs showing and its tread slow and hesitant. The black-and-white man pointed to the back of the cart.

'But, sir ...'

'Ye'll call me Master Jack, not sir. What's wrong?'

'But, sir — I mean, Master Jack — it's dirty.'

Master Jack shouted with what seemed genuine amusement. 'Hark at him!' He cuffed Tom about the ear almost absent-mindedly. 'Ye won't be worrying about a bit o' soot like that tomorrow. Soot means money, and the more o' both the better. Now in with thee, before ye feel my boot.'

Tom climbed into the cart and huddled against the back of the seat. Master Jack hauled a bottle from behind the seat and took a deep swig. He sighed in relief and shoved the bottle back where it came from. Tom heard the flick of the reins, the clop of the horse's hooves. The workhouse slowly disappeared behind them.

chapter five

Murruroo, Australia,
15 April 1868

'Happy birthday, Father! Many happy returns of the day!'

It was Joshua, his muttonchop whiskers neatly trimmed. Thomas had overheard Joshua telling a friend that his father came from 'an old English farming family'. Joshua had always been very careful never to inquire too deeply into his father's past.

Thomas snorted. Joshua, he thought with some amusement, would never see a ghost. He would be afraid it was not the done thing.

'Thank you, Joshua,' he said, as Joshua very correctly gave his father his arm to help him down the stairs.

I don't need help, thought Thomas. But he took the arm anyway. Joshua was a good enough boy.

Thomas grinned to himself. Boy! Joshua was sixty-eight. But Thomas still thought of him as a boy.

Suddenly he realised that Joshua was taking him into the breakfast room. He took his hand from Joshua's arm. 'Thank you, my boy. But I think I'll take the air for a while before I breakfast.'

Joshua stared. He would never think of going for a walk before breakfast. But all he said was, 'As you like, Father. Would you like me to accompany you?'

Yes, he was a good boy, thought Thomas. But so dull. 'No, thank you, Joshua,' he said gently.

Thomas worried sometimes about what would happen to Murruroo after his death. Joshua was capable, but he had no urge to love the land. His son, Thomas's eldest grandson, was the same. And Joshua's younger brother, Marcus — he'd told the family gaily he had no wish to stare at sheep bums all his life and joined the army. He was Captain Marcus Appleby now.

This land has given me so much, thought Thomas. I wish I could know that I will leave it in safe hands when I die.

Thomas walked carefully down the hall and down the stairs to the drive, then turned and crossed the drive onto the neatly mown terrace and looked around.

There was no-one there. Thomas snorted again. What did I expect? he thought. The ghost had probably been Mrs Henderson, checking to see if the windows needed cleaning, or the gardener — what was his name? — checking all looked neat for this afternoon's party.

Thomas turned to look at the house himself. It was a good house. A grand house: eighteen rooms and seven chimneys. Big, solid chimneys they were too, he'd insisted on that. Make them wide and make them straight, he'd said, the sort of chimney you can poke a brush up easily.

Those chimneys gave him almost as much pride as owning 4000 acres. That's where it had all begun, of course, with chimneys, more than eighty years ago.

Thomas turned to go back into the house. As he turned he caught a flash of movement. Someone was in the rose garden, on the other side of the house.

chapter six

London, 1785

There were four of them in the cellar that first night, the soot piled at one end of the cold, damp room, the boys at the other, huddled on empty soot sacks.

Big Bill was the oldest at thirteen. He coughed wetly through the night, his body racked with ulcers from years of soot. He screamed now when he had to pee, and lived most of his life in sullen exhaustion from the pain.

Master Jack ignored the screams mostly, though if he was in a good mood he'd give Bill some gin to dull the agony. But even after seven years of starving, Big Bill was growing. Soon he'd be too large to fit up the chimneys, and after that Master Jack would have no use for him at all.

Little Will was six and mostly silent. Sometimes Tom wondered if he'd been born with half a mind, he was so quiet. Other times he thought the boy had known so few words in his life of dark cellars and darker chimneys that he simply had no words to say.

Jem was a few years older than Tom, but not as large as Bill. He was silent too, but his silence was different.

Jem seemed to assess the world and keep his opinion of it to himself.

But there were no introductions that first night. Tom stumbled down the cellar stairs, half-stupid from hunger and fatigue; he had found the pile of legs and arms almost by instinct. Sleep had been like a hammer blow, as though he had no strength to go further, rather than the gentle softness of sleep at home, and it was dreamless too, as though the memory of home hurt too much even to dream of it.

It felt like he'd only been asleep for a minute when light erupted into the dank room.

'Time to get up, brats.' It was a woman's voice. Tom heard her sniff at the top of the cellar stairs. 'They'd sleep all day and night too left to theyselves, so they would. Look lively now, or there'll be no supper for the lot of ye!'

The arms and legs suddenly separated and turned into boys again. Footsteps hurried to the stairs and disappeared upwards. Tom followed them, confused.

It was hard to see after the dark of the cellar. Tom blinked. The world suddenly cleared. The room had a fireplace, but no fire; a table, splintery and with shaky legs; a lantern; two chairs with mended legs, and a bed piled with coats and dirty blankets.

Chimney brushes, shovels and long rods leant against one wall. The table was piled with broken crockery — cracked mugs, bowls, a jug with half a spout, another with no handle. The smell of dirt and sweat and soot was overpowering.

Master Jack sat at one end of the table. His eyes were shut as he slowly swigged from the brown glass bottle Tom had seen the day before — or one just like it — letting the liquid pour down his throat with a look of curious dedication. Today he wore a long coat roughly tied with string, and another tall black hat with a battered brim.

The woman sat beside him. She was short and squat as an iron pot, her nose and chin as red as Jack's were white. Her feet bulged in tatty slippers. Her legs under the ragged skirt were blotched with purple. She took a gulp from one of the jugs, then set it back on the table with a gasp.

'Needed that,' she puffed. She beckoned Tom towards her, then pinched his chin between her dirty fingers. 'Got some meat on him,' she remarked. 'Well, what's your name then?'

'Tom,' he replied.

'And are ye a good boy, Tom?' She cackled like she'd said something funny, as Big Bill broke into another fit of coughing behind them, then wiped a gob of bloody mucus on his sleeve.

'I try to be,' said Tom.

The woman laughed again. Her breath smelt sour and sweet at the same time. She looked down at Tom's boots, then at his stockings and his breeches.

'Worth a guinea,' she remarked. 'Mebbe more.' She clicked her finger. 'Off with 'em, boy. And you shut up!' she yelled to Bill. 'Fair makes me ears ache to hear ye.'

Tom stared. 'My — my boots?'

'And ye socks and ye britches and ye shirt.'

'But I have no others,' stammered Tom.

Someone grabbed him from behind. It was Master Jack. 'When the missus says off with 'em, you off with 'em, you understand?' Master Jack gave him a casual blow across the face that sent him crashing into the bed across the room.

'And thank ye stars that was me hand and not me whip,' added Master Jack, though there was no anger in his tone. 'Shall we get a few things straight, eh, lad? I am thy master and I will be for seven years. And for seven years ye'll do what I say and when I say or know the reason why. Now strip. Lettice will bring thee sommat else to wear.'

Tom glanced at the three other boys, their faces so thick with dirt it was even more difficult to tell their colour. All three stood back against the wall, Big Bill's hands slowly writhing as they always did from pain; Little Will staring at the food on the table. Only Jem stared at Tom, though his expression told Tom nothing of his thoughts at all.

Tom sat on the floor and slowly pulled off his boots and then his breeches and his socks. He held them out as the woman, Lettice, reached over.

She felt the breeches lovingly. 'Worth 'alf a guinea for the lot of 'em, mebbe,' she gloated as she heaved herself up from the table, Tom's clothes in her hand. She gestured to the boys. 'You, eat if you're goin' to! There be work to be done for some this night.'

The three other boys fell upon the table as though starving, each lifting a cracked and filthy bowl to their lips. After the first gulp Jem hesitated, then handed a similar bowl to Tom.

'Better eat,' he said. His accent was strange, so strange that Tom found the words difficult to understand. But the meaning was clear.

Tom looked at the contents of the bowl. Watery milk, more blue than white and already speckled with yellow, and soggy bread. But suddenly he was too hungry to care.

Tom lifted the bowl and drank, just as Lettice lumbered in with a pile of rags in her arms. She threw them down to him.

The clothes were thin and crusty. Tom put them on anyway. His feet already screamed with cold.

Master Jack grinned at him, then coughed, and spat a gob of mucus on to the floor. 'That's more like,' he said approvingly. 'The chimleys'll know thee now.' He nodded to the three boys, who grabbed the chimney brushes, the rods, the scrapers, the shovels, empty sacks and buckets obediently. 'Let's you say hello to 'em then, shall we?'

chapter seven

London, 1785

It was almost night outside, not the daylight Tom had expected. Chimney sweeps in London often worked at night, when the house-owners were asleep and the fires extinguished.

He had been too tired to notice much before. Now the horror of London struck him like a blow: the high wooden tenements that looked like a gust of wind would knock them down; the flies thick on piles of human excrement; the pigeons scrabbling in the horse dung on the cobbles in the last of the light; and all around the gabble, the street cries and the stench.

'Don't stand there gawping, boy,' said Master Jack.

It was a long walk. No-one spoke, unless you counted Bill's wet coughs or the gulping as Master Jack swigged from the bottle in his pocket. Tom felt the filth of the street ooze cold between his toes. He couldn't stand this. He couldn't!

But he had to. Tom shut his eyes for a second and felt the courage cloak wrap around him again. He opened his eyes and walked on.

The streets were narrow and made narrower still by food stalls selling chestnuts and hot potatoes (the smell made Tom's head swim with hunger), sprawled drunks — or were they dead or sleeping, their bottles of gin still clasped in their hands? — women with thin faces and ragged shawls and a look of desperate invitation to any man that passed. The houses loomed above them, so it was only possible to see the smallest stretch of smoky sky between them.

It was a world of shadows, black clothes, brown cobbles, shadows and the ever-present coal fog, thick in some streets, thin in others, but always choking at your lungs, as though London grudged you every breath you took.

Finally the streets grew wider as the night grew darker. Master Jack stopped and prodded the boys down a lane and up a flight of stairs.

It was a big house, though nowhere near the size of the magistrate's back home; a tradesman's house, perhaps. They entered through the back door and trod on sacks the housemaid put down before them to keep their sooty feet from the floor.

'The master and missus are from home,' said the cook. 'But mind ye leave no mess. If there's mess I ain't paying,' she added to Jack.

The small party stopped in the kitchen first, while Master Jack fitted the rods into one of the brushes.

'Up ye go, boy,' he said heartily to Little Will, handing the child a soot scraper as well.

The boy placed his tiny hand on the wall by the kitchen chimney. ''Tis still too hot,' he mumbled. ''Twill burn me up.'

'All the better on a cold night,' said Jack with a grin at the cook. 'Scamper up there and there won't be time to burn. And there'll be plum cake for thee at the top.'

The small boy gave him a look of disbelief, then clambered surprisingly quickly into the hearth. In two swift movements he'd braced his legs against one side of the hearth, his back against the other, and wriggled upwards. Master Jack leant into the chimney and handed him the brush and soot scraper.

Tom had some knowledge of chimney sweeping from home. They'd had their chimney swept a time or two that he remembered. The smallest of the boys was always sent up the kitchen chimney, which was usually the narrowest in the house, with fat and grease mixed with its soot. Tom had never paid much attention, never thought what it must be like for the boys, there in the heat and darkness of the chimney.

Now, it seemed, he was about to find out.

Master Jack gave another too-friendly grin to the cook. 'Any chance of a pint o' porter, missus? Me throat's that parched.'

'No,' said the cook.

Jack shrugged, as though he hadn't really expected it, and spread his sacks to catch the soot that Will scraped down. They made their way to the parlour. The room was dark except for the candle the cook carried. The sparse light gleamed on brocade and polished furniture.

Big Bill was moaning, an almost unconscious moan as though his body dreaded what was to come. Master Jack pinched his ear, hard. 'You stoppen that!' he hissed.

Big Bill paid no attention, his eyes fixed on the wide parlour fireplace. But he stopped moaning. Master Jack handed him the chimney brush as Bill fitted his lanky shape into the hearth and began to edge upwards. Again the boys waited while Jack fixed the bags for the soot, then the cook led the way out of the parlour and up the stairs.

This room was a bedroom. The fireplace was wide but the room was cold.

'Now ye turn,' said Master Jack to Tom. 'An easy one fer yer first go. Let's see what thou can do.' He shrugged a shoulder at Jem. ''E'll show yer the first time. After that it's up to you.'

Tom closed his eyes for a second, frantically weighing his choices. If he dodged out the door he could run so far that Jack couldn't find him, find a printer perhaps who'd apprentice him to the trade in spite of his lack of years. Even now he had no thought of begging for help. He'd learnt already that most were too concerned with their own lives to help another.

Jack seemed to guess what he was thinking. 'Try to run and I'll strip the hide off yer back,' he said to Tom, then added to Jem, 'Take yer shirt off.'

Jem obeyed wordlessly, his eyes on Tom.

Tom gazed at Jem's back. It was a mess of red and pink and raised white scars.

'That's what 'appens to boys that don't obey their masters,' said Jack with satisfaction. 'And then the Black Man gets 'em too.' He grinned at Tom's look of bewilderment. 'Ye don't know the Black Man? Lives in chimleys, 'e does, and 'e sucks the blood out of bad boys and spits their bones all down the chimley. Now, up with youse.'

Jem went first, wedging his way up with the ease of long practice. Tom followed more slowly.

The first minute was the worst, trying to find a way to balance with his back against one wall and his feet against the other. Then suddenly the pattern fell into place. It was like walking, Tom decided, but sideways.

One step, two steps, inch your body up. Another step, and another, and move your back again. The sharp edges of the soot and brick and the thin, ragged ledges of mortar bit into his skin. His feet yelled with pain.

The chimney brush was pushed up after him. 'Ye'll need to pull that after ye,' said Jack. 'Or ye'll have to do it all again.'

Up, up, up ... the soot fell as Jem dislodged it above him. Tom closed his eyes. There was no need to keep them open: there was no light with which to see.

Up, up ... up ... Suddenly one of his feet inched into nothingness. Tom almost fell, but caught himself in time.

'Should've warned ye,' said Jem. It was the first time Tom had heard him speak since they'd entered the chimney. His voice echoed strangely in the darkness of the chimney. 'It branches 'ere.'

'Branches?'

'Two chimneys meet. Twist around a way. That's it. Ye needs take care when they branch. Sweeps 'ave been lost afore this.'

'Lost?' asked Tom.

'Wander the chimneys forevermore,' said Jem gleefully. 'Till the rats eat 'em. Then their ghosts wander instead. Hear 'em howling, sometimes, the ghosts.'

Tom gulped. 'Will we meet rats?'

'Here? Nah. Only old chimleys where ye meet rats. Big as a dog sometimes, they are. Meet rats like that and ye'll never see the light again.'

'What about the Black Man?'

'Never seen 'im. Not yet anyways.' Jem's rush of information stopped as suddenly as it had begun. Again the boys moved upwards, stopping to use their scrapers on the ledges or where the soot had baked too hard for the brushes to shift.

How far had they gone? Tom wondered desperately. Surely they were near the top now? He couldn't breathe, his legs were agony, his back felt like another step would break it.

And suddenly, out of nowhere, a blackness descended over his soul, and he hated Pa with all his heart — Pa who had printed the pamphlet that had led to his death, Pa who had left him all alone, left him to the chimneys and the bitter taste of soot . . .

Then all at once there was light above, the red gleam of a star, and not the solid blackness of Jem's body. Tom could smell the air now, the stale smoke-laden air of London that smelt fresh after the bitter fug inside the chimney.

A dirty hand reached down and helped him out. 'Ye did well enough for the first,' said Jem grudgingly. 'All the way up too and no screaming. Sometimes the master 'as to light a fire under the new ones to get 'em to go up. That's what 'e did with Dick. Lit a fire till 'is heels blistered. Dick moved up all right then.'

Tom stared around. They were on the slope of a roof, wedged between the tiles and the chimney. The stars looked cold and clean above them. Below, rooftops gleamed, with here and there the yellow glow of a window lit by candles or a lamp. 'Which one is Dick?' asked Tom.

'Nah, Dick's dead. Got stuck up a chimley, 'e did. Couldn't get 'im out. Some fool lit a fire to try to smoke 'im out afore Master could get the ropes to pull 'im, an' he died of the smoke. That's why the master went to fetch you when 'e sold the soot, to take Dick's place.'

'Where does he sell the soot?'

'To farmers.'[1] Jem spat on his hands as though to clean them. 'Come on. We'd better get on down or Master'll 'ave our hides.'

The next chimney Tom did on his own, dragging the giant brush behind him, or pushing it in front of him

---

[1]Soot was used as fertiliser.

when the way was too blocked for his body to push past, hearing the soot fall with soft thuds into the bags below. He was almost beyond pain and fear — or tiredness or hunger — now. There was just the dim consciousness that he was still alive, that his body could still put one foot after another, drag his back up another inch at a time.

The cook was waiting for them in the kitchen. She thrust a mug of porter at Master Jack, then handed each of the boys a bun.

'Eat it quick,' muttered Jem. 'The master don't like to see us eat. If'n we grow too big we don't fit in the chimleys.'

It hurt his lips to eat, but Tom ate it anyway. Everything hurt, but that dim voice inside that said he lived also told him to eat.

There was cheese inside the bun, and apple, and the top was sticky with something sweet. But Tom's body was only aware that it was food.

Going home was worse. They had to carry the sacks of soot, Little Will with one and the others each with two, weighing them down till they were bent almost double, and Tom thought again of Pa's body contorted in the stocks.

Master Jack's face was whiter than ever and his swigs at the bottle more frequent. Finally they slipped the bags from their backs at the bottom of the cellar stairs.

'That's the lot, then,' said Master Jack in relief.

Tom wondered if he would call them up the stairs for supper, or breakfast, or whatever meal was due now.

But he simply staggered up the stairs. Tom heard the bolt shoved roughly in the door.

'Over 'ere,' said someone. Tom tried to place the voice. It was Jem.

Tom staggered over to the others on the mound of sacks and sank down. Until that day he had never slept with others before, but he knew that without their body warmth within minutes his body would be too chilled to sleep. There were fewer sacks now, too. Master Jack must have sold his load of soot the day he'd bought Tom at the workhouse and come home with his bags empty.

Now some of them were full of soot again. Tom guessed that as the week went by there'd be even fewer sacks to lie on.

Something scuttled so close to him he felt the air move against his skin. 'What was that?' he cried.

'Just a rat.' It was Jem's voice, already half asleep. 'Don't give it no mind. We're bigger'n it is. Might give ye a nip if ye roll off by yerself, but.'

Tom shrank back into the huddle of the others. I'm a rat now, he thought. Living in cellars and chimneys, eating scraps and frightened of anyone who's bigger than me — like Master Jack. But I won't be frightened. I refuse. If I hadn't been frightened Pa might still be alive. There might be a way out of this, too.

He tried to imagine the courage cloak again, all red and warm about him. It helped a bit, though not much. Finally Tom slept.

chapter eight

London, 1785

The days passed, unseen by the boys in the cellar. They were creatures of the night, locked in till dusk in case the light spoilt their night vision, starved to keep them small, worked throughout the night, then brought back to sleep among the soot, their nights broken by Bill's coughs or moans.

Tom learnt to scrape off the oil crust that stuck to the chimneys' edges, as well as brush the soot away. He learnt how to mortar crumbling chimneys, how to leap down from chimney tops onto sloping roofs without falling to his death. He learnt how to shove his brush at the rats, or lash out with his fist. The rats' eyes gleamed, their teeth were sharp, but if you refused to be frightened they ran away.

Once Master Jack set him to putting out a chimney fire that had burnt for two days, creeping up the baking walls with rags wrapped round his face and feet and hands, and a ragged hat upon his head, poking at the burning soot with his brush till it fell in smouldering embers all about him, down into the fireplace below.

The burning soot left sores on his face and arms, but the cook was pleased and gave him a whole plum pudding. Master Jack took most of it, but Tom still got a hefty slice and the others got crumbs of it too.

Then one morning Master Jack kept Big Bill back when the others crept down the cellar stairs to sleep. When Tom woke the boy was gone.

'Where is he?' Tom hissed to Jem as they trod up the cellar stairs.

Jem shrugged. 'Worked 'is seven year, 'e 'as,' he muttered. 'Master got rid of 'im. 'Im and 'is cough and 'is moaning. Getting too big for the chimleys Bill was, anyways.'

'But where has he gone?'

'Workhouse, mebbe.' Jem spoke as though it was no concern of his where the boy he'd shared his life with had gone.

That night it was a larger house — two fireplaces in the kitchen alone. Master Jack sent Will to the kitchens, as usual, and Jem and Tom to the chimneys on the floors above.

It was the most complex set of chimneys Tom had encountered yet. His chimney took the smoke from two fireplaces on the first floor and then another four on the floor above, and two above that as well.

Tom found it hard to keep the way straight in his mind, up there in the soot and darkness, the eight chimney tunnels leading into each other. Twice he lost the way and tried to climb where there was no way out.

It was difficult to tell which way truly led out when the chimneys were so clogged up with soot, and he felt the panic of every chimney sweep deep in his mind, that somehow he would wander there in the sharp-edged darkness forever, till the last glimmer of his life dissolved.

But finally there was fresh air above him. Tom jumped down from the chimney, hoping as he did each time that he wouldn't slip on the mossy tiles and crash to his death, then he made his way down the ladder that leant against the roof, his brushes on his shoulder, and crept back into the scullery, trying to practise a smile. If you smiled right at a cook, and muttered 'Yes'm' when she told you to mind her clean floors, most times she'd give you a bite to eat. Last week it had even been plum cake, all moist and rich, and the day before a bit of cheese.

There was no sign of Master Jack or Will in the scullery, or kitchen either. A tired scullery maid nodded her head to the servants' stairs. 'They be up there,' she said with a yawn.

Tom hesitated. 'Would you have a crust of bread, miss?' he asked hopefully. 'I'm that famished.'

The housemaid stared. 'Cook said I was to see ye didn't filch nothing.'

'Maybe she didn't mean food,' pleaded Tom.

The girl looked at him a moment more. 'I've a brother ye age,' she said suddenly. 'Haven't seen 'im since last year. He's not going to be a sweep though. Got a job with the farmer, 'e has, like our dad. Here.' She moved to the meat safe in the middle of the room and took out a dish of mutton, the cold meat congealing in its fat. She put a fresh loaf and a dish of butter next to it. 'I'll keep an eye out for cook 'n' your master,' she whispered. 'Eat it quickly while ye can.'

Tom stared at the meat. It was the first he'd seen in over a month. He grasped the bone and began to tear off the meat with his teeth, ignoring the pain from the soot sores on his lips and tongue.

'Not like that!' hissed the girl. 'Oh, well, never mind, I'll say the cat got at it! Here.' She cut him a slab of bread and piled on the butter.

Tom ate till he could eat no more. The girl looked at him sympathetically. 'Thought you looked half-starved,' she began, when a bellow at the door interrupted them.

'Tom! Where is that boy? Tom!'

Tom ran for the door and up the servants' stairs. Master Jack gave him a careless cuff about the ear.

'That Jem's got hisself stuck,' he said shortly. ''Alf the world can hear 'im screaming.'

Tom listened. Now he could hear Jem too, a muffled scream far above them deep inside the chimney. 'Why can't he get out?' he asked.

Master Jack shrugged. 'Got hisself wedged in a corner, see, where one chimley meets another.'

Tom nodded. Bends were the most difficult of all, especially as you grew taller. You could get your head through and bend your body around the curve. But legs didn't bend except in one direction, and once you were stuck you could go neither forward nor back.

'Up ye go after 'im,' said Master Jack. 'See if ye can pull 'im down.'

Tom wedged himself into the chimney and edged himself upwards. It was easy going now that Jem had swept the way clear before him. Up, up ... suddenly the chimney branched and twisted where another joined it. And Tom felt Jem's feet touch his head in the darkness.

'Jem?'

'Who else did ye think it'd be?' Jem's voice was high and shrill. He sounded younger.

'I'm going to pull your legs downwards.'

No answer. Tom took the silence for a yes. He grasped one of the calloused feet and pulled.

Jem screamed as his body was pulled against the ledge of the chimney. But he still stayed stuck.

Tom pulled again, managing to grasp both feet this time.

Still no movement.

'Tom?'

'What?'

Jem's voice was pleading. 'Don't let 'em break me back. Please don't let 'em break me back.'

'I won't,' promised Tom, though both boys knew that it would be Master Jack who decided. He pulled again. Nothing happened except the quick-drawn scream of pain.

'It's no use!' Master Jack's voice boomed up the chimney. 'Come on down, lad. We'll try a rope on 'im next.'

Tom slithered down. Master Jack was already gathering the ropes. Little Will watched him expressionlessly.

''Ere.' Master Jack passed Tom the rope. 'Tie that round 'is feet and come back down. We'll pull together.'

'Won't it hurt him?' ventured Tom.

Master Jack grunted. 'Mebbe. Mebbe not.'

Tom stared at him. The food helped him think more clearly. That must be what Jem had meant, up there in the chimney. If they pulled his legs with too much force and he was hopelessly jammed, his back might break. He'd die, or at best be crippled; a life of begging if he was lucky, a slow death if he wasn't.

Master Jack muttered under his breath as he untangled the ropes. 'No pain in heaven. Boy'd be lucky to end it like this. To think of it, no pain.' His face was even whiter today, and sometimes he gave a moan like Bill's.

Tom tried to think. Chimney sweeps were cheap — Master Jack could buy another for what the customer would give him for this one chimney. But the customer would give Jack nothing if the chimney was blocked by the body of a dead or dying chimney sweep.

That's all Jem would be, Tom thought bitterly. A blockage in the chimney, so the smoke couldn't escape.

'Please,' he said quickly. 'Can I try something else?'

Jack stared. 'What?'

'If I climbed onto the roof and down the chimney I might be able to scrape some of the soot off the ledge where Jem is caught. That might make the hole bigger and he could get out.'

Master Jack considered. 'Worth a try,' he said grudgingly, obviously comparing the time wasted trying to get Jem out with the time he'd have to take buying another boy. He made a decision. 'Look lively then,' he ordered. 'And thee,' he said to Will, who was staring vacantly about him as though this was no concern of his. 'Stop staring like a lovesick pigeon and start sweeping up the mess 'ere.'

Tom ran, the soot scraper in his hand. Down the stairs again, out to the yard, up the ladder. For a moment he hesitated, wondering which was the right chimney. Finally he edged over to the nearest, hauled up the ladder so he could climb it, and called down. 'Jem! Can you hear me?'

'Yes!'

Tom let out a sigh of relief. 'I'm coming down. Watch out! I'll be bringing soot down with me.'

'Aye!'

Tom lowered his legs into the chimney and paused. It was more difficult getting into position here, with no floor to brace himself against. For a moment he was afraid he'd plummet all the way down to where Jem was trapped and the two of them would die, not just the one. But it was easier to brace himself than he'd feared.

Tom began to inch his way down.

Lower, lower . . .

'Stop!'

'Jem?'

'Yer right on me head.'

'Can I stand?' demanded Tom.

'Mebbe. There's a ledge beside ye. It's narrow, but.'

Tom lowered himself slowly, feeling with his feet till the ledge was firm beneath him. He crouched down. 'I'm going to try to scrape off the soot on either side of you. You try scraping, too. Then maybe there'll be room to move.'

There was a silence, then Jem said, 'It be worth a try.' There was hope in his voice now.

Tom began to scrabble in the soot. It was almost impossibly difficult, balanced in the darkness of the narrow, soot-encrusted ledge, the soot baked like stone so that shards pierced his skin, despite his new callouses. Beside him Jem scrabbled too, digging his scraper into the hard-baked muck, then pushing it down the chimney. Finally Tom's fingertips felt brick instead of soot.

'Jem? I think we've moved all that we can.'

Tom felt, rather than saw, Jem nod below. 'Can you wriggle sideways?'

Jem's body lurched beside him, but again it didn't move.

'No!' Jem's voice was growing desperate once more.

'I'll try to push you down.' Tom thought for a moment, then he wedged both feet against Jem's shoulders and braced his hands against the chimney wall. He shoved downwards, as hard as he could, and felt Jem's body jerk suddenly sideways.

Jem gasped with pain. 'Sorry,' said Tom.

'Keep goin',' muttered Jem hoarsely.

Tom nodded, though he knew the other boy couldn't see him. He reached down and grabbed Jem's hands. 'I'm going to pull upwards instead,' he said. 'Can you sort of wriggle at the same time?'

'Aye.'

Tom pulled. For a moment he thought it wouldn't work. Then suddenly Jem began to move, slowly and painfully, over the lip that held him.

Jem screamed again, but this time the cry had as much triumph as pain in it.

'Can you make it out the chimney?' asked Tom worriedly.

'I can make it.'

Tom began to work his way upwards again, listening to the sounds of Jem below. Then suddenly he was up there, into the blessed air, reaching down to haul Jem the last few feet.

They were free.

chapter nine

London, 1785

Later, in the damp blackness of the cellar, Jem whispered, 'Y' awake?'

'Yes,' Tom answered softly. Beside them little Will snored with the moist snorts of one whose nose was choked with soot. Tom waited for Jem to say the thanks he hadn't said before, as the boys had made their slow and painful way down the ladder to Master Jack's cuffs and complaints that they had robbed him of a half-day's work.

Now Jem said, 'If ye had anything, anything ye wanted, what'd it be?'

Tom tried to think, but all he could see was the life that he'd once had, Pa and their shop and the quiet rooms above, and Mistress Foggerty on Tuesdays to do the washing and make stew. Finally he said, 'I don't know.'

Jem snorted. 'If ye dunno know what ye want, ye'll die, get drowned in soot.'

'What do you want, then?' demanded Tom.

'Me? I want a flower barrow.' Jem's voice was suddenly passionate. 'Seen 'em in Covent Garden.

Barrows filled with flowers as sweet as Heaven and the toffs come and pays ye money for each one. That's what I want.'

Tom was silent. It seemed to him that Jem's dream was as far away as his.

'Whatcher thinkin'?' demanded Jem.

'That there's no way to find your dream,' said Tom honestly.

Jem gave a short laugh in the darkness. 'You're wrong there, me cob.' He hesitated. 'Can I trust ye?'

'Yes,' said Tom.

'I reckon I can an' all,' said Jem. 'Most coves would've left me 'anging there today. You follow me.'

Jem wriggled across to the other corner of the floor and grappled with something. Tom followed. He heard a grating sound. Then Jem said, 'Grab hold o' me shirt then.'

There was a hole and sudden light. Tom blinked.

They were in another cellar, but this one was empty, the floor above rotted away and half open to the foggy sky.

For the first time in a month Tom stood in daylight, or the yellow smog that was all that Londoners knew.

Jem grinned. 'This ain't all. Come on.'

'Master Jack . . .?'

'He's drunk or asleep or both, and Lettice too.' Jem looked around furtively, in case someone was peering in the cellar, then ran over to the far wall. He shoved a brick away with his foot. 'There!' he said proudly.

Tom knelt and stared into the hole in the brickwork. Something gleamed inside. He reached to touch it. Jem hauled his hand back. 'No touching! 'Sides, someone might see.' He shoved the brick back swiftly.

'What is it?'

'Things.' He stared at Tom for a second then added, 'A pocket watch and two 'andkerchiefs and a brooch. Reckon they's worth twenty quid or more. Other things too.'

'Whose are they?'

'Mine,' Jem said indignantly, then added, 'Now.'

'You mean you stole them,' said Tom slowly.

'I mean they're mine!' said Jem fiercely. 'I mean, them as I took 'em from won't miss 'em. An' I'll get me barrow, an' it'll be soon, 'cause I'm growin', an' next time I gets stuck mebbe ye won't be there to help me.'

He looked at Tom sideways. 'Could be your barrow too, if ye wants. 'Nother watch, a ring or two. We can sneak off, you an' me, go where Master can't find us. Find a pawnbroker, sell the goods, we'll 'ave it made.' He stared at Tom. 'Ye with me?'

Tom thought of the chimneys, the magistrate's face as he condemned him to the workhouse, Master Jack, the boys who'd pelted Pa with turds. They had stolen his father, his few possessions, his freedom, his life . . .

'I'm with you,' he announced, and felt the hate and hope blossom in his heart.

London, 1785

Jem's mother had been a barmaid. He'd never known his father.

'Did he die?' asked Tom cautiously.

Jem shrugged. 'Ma never knew who 'e was, most like.'

Tom absorbed the knowledge silently. In his village children had come with marriage; or if they hadn't, marriage was soon arranged by the church wardens. But London was a different world.

'I thought you might be Master Jack's son.'

Jem gave a bark of laughter. ''Im? 'E'll never have no son. The soot's got 'is cods, like it got Bill's. Reckon Bill's had it, though, 'e's got the soot cough too. That's why old Jack sent 'im to the workhouse. Bill'll be in 'is coffin by Michaelmas.' Jem seemed quite unconcerned about Bill's fate.

'Where's your ma, then?' Tom hesitated. 'Mine died of typhus,' he added.

Jem shrugged. 'Drunk under a bridge, mebbe. That's why she sold me to Jack, to get the drink. Bad luck to 'er.'

'She sold you!' Tom hesitated. 'How much for?'

'Fifteen shillings,' said Jem, with a touch of pride. 'More'n 'e paid for any of the others. What did he give the workhouse for you?'

'Twelve shillings,' said Tom quickly. It was a lie, but the only present he could think to give to one who was offering him a future.

Jem nodded with satisfaction. 'Twelve shillings is still a good price,' he said generously. ''E only gave six shillings for Will.'

Tom nodded at the hidden cache. 'How do we get them?'

'How do you think? Look,' said Jem, 'most chimleys are fed by two fires, right? Or more sometimes. Old Jack, 'e sends us up one. But I go down the other chimley, climbs out the fireplace into the other room, looks round, sees something I can sell. I ties it under me shirt and up I goes again. Easy peasy.'

'But what if we're caught?' whispered Tom.

'Who's to catch us? Most times there's nubbut home save a slavey or two. Rich folks don't want soot in their catlap. We goes in when they're away with other rich folks some place. An' if there's someone there when ye come out the fireplace, ye say all polite like, "pardon milord or lady", stuff like that, and whip back up the chimley.

'But you've got to be careful, like,' Jem added. 'Don' take sommat they'll miss. That watch, I found it under a chair along of dust so thick it'd need a chimley brush. I reckon someone lost it weeks before, an' no-one'd miss it now. Slow and careful, that's the way to do it. 'Ere.'

He looked around, reached into the cache again, then handed Tom a lump of rags.

'What are these for?'

'Stuff 'em in ye breeches and tie a bit around yer face when you go up the chimley, but secret, so Master can't see. That soot, it gets into yer cods 'n' eyes 'n' things. Eats 'em away. That's what it did t' Bill.'

Tom hesitated. 'You never told Bill about this?'

'Bill? Nah.' Jem looked scornful. 'Bill'd blab it first chance 'e got. But yer all right. Spit on it, eh?'

'What?'

'Like this.' Jem spat on his hand, then held it out. Tom spat too and held his hand to Jem's.

'Spit for gold and spit to hold. Let me die iffen I tell a lie. Brothers, right?'

'Brothers,' agreed Tom.

'An' if you split on me,' Jem added carelessly, 'I'll cut yer tongue out while ye sleeps.'

'I won't split,' said Tom.

Jem glanced at him. 'Nah,' he said. 'Didn't think ye would. If ye were that sort of cove ye'd never have risked yer neck fer me back in the chimley.'

Now, in the moments before exhausted sleep, Tom dreamt of flowers again. Not the flowers in the hedges at home — white hawthorn, pink briar — but flowers of all shapes and colours in the barrow they'd keep at Covent Garden; flowers that smelt like home. And maybe they'll sell cabbages too, said Jem, or potatoes, and they'd take the spoilt ones home each night and boil them for their supper, as many as they could eat …

The hoard grew slowly. Jem managed a handkerchief that first week, a good silk one worth at least a guinea or more, and a few days later Tom stole a silver spoon from the scullery when the maid's back was turned. It was his first theft, and he was proud of it, and polished the spoon against his rags before they slid it behind the bricks, and every night Tom dreamt of his spoon shining in the darkness, waiting for them, and the growing collection that would buy their freedom.

Autumn came, though there were no trees near their cellar to change colour. But sometimes by lamplight Tom saw the gold of autumn leaves in the streets where they cleaned the chimneys, and knew that the year was turning.

Winter, and his feet turned blue and his fingers, too. Jem showed him how to wrap rags from worn-out coal sacks around his feet. The rags were soon soaked in the mud and slush, but they helped a bit.

Christmas came, only noticed as there were no chimneys to clean that day, and the boys were kept locked in the cellar for two days and nights while Master Jack had the luxury of nothing to do but drink and sing and drink again, to try to ease the constant pain from a lifetime of the soot.

Tom slept most of Christmas Eve and night. There was always too little time for sleep, broken by cold and pain and coughing or the inquisitive rats that clambered over them, hoping for food or nesting places amid the huddled limbs of the boys.

Late Christmas Day, though, he woke to find Jem nudging him. He sat up, blinking instinctively to try to make out what was in front of him, though there was no light at all to see by in the cellar. 'Here, get yer dabblers round this,' urged Jem.

Something hot was shoved into Tom's hand. He clutched it automatically, revelling in the warmth.

'What is it?'

'Hot potato.' Tom could hear rather than see Jem's grin. 'One for each of us.' His arm went out to feel where Little Will was, and Bertie, the four year old who had taken Bill's place.

Tom didn't ask where they had come from, not with Will and Bertie to hear. Jem must have crept out of the cellar to their hiding place, and swapped one of their pieces of stolen loot for the potatoes.

It put their dream of a flower barrow further away, but with the warmth of the potato in his hand, Tom didn't care. It was Christmas, after all. He nibbled the potato slowly, to make it last, huddled with the others in their nest of sacks.

One day, he thought, as the last of the potato's heat faded from his fingers, one day Jem and I will have hot potatoes every night, and morning too. We'll see the sunlight every day and never see the night at all, except to sleep. A life of sun and flowers ...

The next day he stole a knife and a ring from an old lady, while she slept, and carried them wrapped in rags against his body up the chimney.

chapter eleven

London, 1786

The last of the grey winter slush was melting in the streets when Jem got stuck again. Tom chipped at the hard-baked soot with his fingers, and when that failed wrenched a brick from the crumbling chimney.

It took two hours to free him. Jem's face was white when Tom had finished, and Master Jack was swearing. That night he whipped all four boys. It was the first time Tom had been whipped, though Jack had cuffed him a few times. Compared to many, Master Jack was none too bad a master. The whipping hardly broke the skin.

Later, in the cellar, Jem nudged Tom awake. They crept out through the hole in the cellar wall and into the sunlight.

'Hurt?' asked Jem.

'Hardly at all,' lied Tom, feeling his shirt stick to his bloody skin.

Jem nodded. He was silent for a moment, so Tom wondered what was wrong. Then Jem said, 'We 'ave to make a break for it. Tomorrow night. Can't wait any longer.'

Tom blinked, in shock as well as from the foggy sunlight. 'Why?'

'Second time I've been stuck,' said Jem. 'I'm too big now, that's the trouble. Master'll get rid of me soon enough, 'n then I'm for the workhouse. Be the devil's own job t' break outer there.'

Tom gazed at him; Jem was right. Despite the cruel work and starvation he had grown two inches in the past few months, his legs and arms like broomsticks poking from their rags.

'Tomorrow,' said Jem hoarsely. 'We do our work, but don't you sleep once we 'it the cellar. We wait till the others are asleep, then run.'

'Where to?'

Jem shrugged. 'Far as we can. Hole up for a week, two weeks mebbe, till Jack stops looking for us. 'Tis you 'e'll look for anyways, not me, and mayhap 'e won't look too 'ard at that. We sell our stuff piece by piece, and then we buys our barrow.' Jem gulped, as though he, too, found it hard to believe they were so near freedom and their dream. He was silent a moment, then just said, 'Tomorrow.'

'Tomorrow,' agreed Tom. He hesitated, then spat on his hand again, and once more felt Jem's hand in his.

chapter twelve

London, 1786

The last set of chimneys Tom would ever climb belonged to a public house, barely a half-hour walk from their cellar down near the stinking river that served as a sewer and drinking water for three million people. The public house was shambling rooms around a central quadrangle, where thin horses drank from a cracked water trough or pulled hungrily at mouldy hay.

Unlike their other jobs this was to be done in daylight, in the early morning when the night's customers had left or were too drunk to notice a cold hearth. One of the chimneys needed mending, as well as cleaning. Jem carried the wooden bucket of lime mortar as well as his share of the rods and brushes.

The chimneys were simple affairs, straight-up-and-downers, as Jem whispered to Tom when they left Will and Bertie in the fat-slimed kitchens. Tom felt sudden relief. There was less chance of Jem getting stuck in a straight-up-and-downer.

Jem's was the taproom chimney, which was fed from a fireplace in one of the bedrooms too. He had to patch up the crumbling bricks as well as sweep it.

The publican's wife watched suspiciously as Jem mixed water into the bucket of lime mix, swirling it till it was a thick slurry.

''E know what 'e's doin'?' she demanded of Master Jack.

Master Jack smiled his reassuring-customers grin, the one that showed his four remaining teeth. 'Sure he does, missus,' he assured her. 'Trained 'im from a babe, I did. Trained 'im like me own son.'

Tom glanced at Jem. Jem met his eyes. But both had the sense not to grin.

''E'll fix that chimley like it were new,' promised Master Jack.

Tom's was the parlour chimney. It was narrower and was also fed by a pair of bedrooms on the top floor.

Tom stuck his head up the chimney and peered upwards. This chimney looked as though it had been cleaned no more than a few years back, for which Tom was grateful. Some chimneys were so thickly crusted it took all his strength to poke or pull the brush, dislodging layer after layer to clatter sharply into the hearth below. Master Jack hated old soot too. The sharp edges of the slabs of creosote tore holes in his sacks and, besides, the farmers to whom he sold the sackfuls hated creosote. They wanted soft soot that they could spread easily to feed their fields.

Tom braced himself and began to ascend, and suddenly it all seemed real. This was the last chimney he'd ever climb!

Tomorrow, he thought, life will be different. I will never have to breathe the sooty air again. Never feel it cake around my lungs, never fear again the rats above me, the starlings nesting in unused chimney pots, the bats ...

Freedom! The thought made him giddy.

Up, up, up ... It was all so easy today, as though for once an angel flew overhead and said, 'Today it will all go right.'

It's an omen, thought Tom as he looked up and saw a flash of blue between the black. A gust of wind must have shifted the fog for once. Blue sky above him, daylight for the rest of his life ...

Something black loomed on one side. It was the entrance to the bedroom fireplace. Tom shoved his brush in front of him, to push the soot away, and heard it fall soft into the hearth below.

No need to push in any further with the brush, but there might be a chance to pick up some loot in the room beyond. Tom turned himself around, then slid as much as clambered out onto the first-floor fireplace.

No-one yelled, or screamed. So far, so good. Tom dusted the worst of the soot from his shoulders and hair, and looked around.

It was a bedroom, as he'd thought, holding a narrow bed with a single torn, stained blanket and a cracked commode.

The bed was occupied. A man lay there, drool trickling from his mouth as he snored, a gin bottle cuddled against his side.

Drunk, thought Tom. He cleared his throat, then coughed softly.

The man didn't stir.

Safe, then ... Tom crept across the room and gazed down at the sleeping man. No bulge of a watch in his fob pocket, no rings on his fingers. He wore a neckerchief, true, but surely he would wake if Tom tried to untie it.

What of his pockets then? Could he risk it? Or would the man wake up?

He looked too dead drunk to stir. Tom bit his lip. He'd risk it.

Tom stole his hand slowly into the man's pocket. A handkerchief. He pulled it out as slowly as he could, then gasped as something rolled onto the floor. The clink sounded as loud as a shot. Tom glanced again at the man on the bed, but still he didn't sir.

Tom looked down. Coins lay in the dust below the bed. Two sixpences, a threepenny bit, a halfpenny and a guinea! A whole guinea! Tom stared at it. It would be enough to rent them a room, enough so they could eat all the potatoes they wanted till it was safe to find a pawnbroker to buy some of their cache.

The man muttered something and rolled over. Tom shrank back, then bolted for the safety of the chimney, the handkerchief and money clenched in his hand. He waited till he was a good way up before he tied the coins into the handkerchief, then reached down to the rags tied ready around his chest and fumbled the package into them.

Up ... up ... up ... Tom clambered out of the top of the chimney and pulled his brush up after him, giving it another few pokes for luck. The soot caked worst as it cooled, which meant the tops of chimneys were more thickly crusted than the bottoms.

Tom had jumped down the chimney stack and was steadying the ladder when he heard the crash below. Someone screamed; another person shouted. Tom shrugged and checked the coins were safe. Any quarrels going on downstairs had nothing to do with him.

He found Will and Bertie gulping dregs of stale porter from the mugs left to be washed in the hotel scullery. Tom took one and sniffed it, then gulped it too. It smelt bad and tasted worse, but food and drink were too precious to waste. He looked around for scraps, and found some bread and gnawed it. Tomorrow he and Jem would eat hot potatoes and chestnuts too. Maybe a pie ... his mouth watered at the thought.

'Tom! Where is the brat? Show ye heels and get thee 'ere!'

There was no point upsetting Master Jack now. Tom ran, gulping the last of the bread as he did so.

Master Jack was in the taproom. He was sweating, his face even whiter than usual. The landlady stood with him. 'It's not my fault,' she was saying. 'You should have seen to it — it's your business, not mine. And now we'll 'ave to 'ave the constable.'

There were crumbled bricks in the fireplace, and soot too. The dust hovered above the hearth and made it hard to see. There was something else in the fireplace too. At first Tom thought it was just a pile of rags. And then he saw a flash of flesh.

Tom ran forward, knelt in the dust and frantically began to shift the stones from Jem's thin body. But even before he began he knew it was no use.

Jem was dead.

'Not my fault the chimney collapsed,' the woman repeated. 'If you'd known your business it wouldn't 'ave 'appened! And what the constable will say . . .'

'No need for the constable.' Master Jack's voice was curt. 'The brat's dead and there was no man's 'and what did it. Get someone to dump 'im in the river tonight.'

The woman's eyes darted around the room. Then she nodded. She shoved her chin towards Tom. ''E won't say nothin'?'

'Not 'im,' promised Jack. ''E'll keep mum if 'e knows what's good for 'im.' He raised his hand towards Tom, still kneeling by Jem's body.

Tom ducked away. 'I'll keep mum,' he promised. He brushed some of the dust from Jem's face, then felt Master Jack tug at his wrist.

'No time for that now,' Jack muttered. 'Best be out of 'ere. I reckons you've got hands enough to move the body, missus.'

The woman nodded, as Tom thought, Jem — he's just a body now. Like Pa. Jem's body lying still, as though the Black Man who haunted the chimneys had sucked out his life.

Tom's hands unconsciously strayed to the coins nestled against his chest. They were still there, hard and warm.

chapter thirteen

Murruroo, Australia, 15 April 1868

'Happy birthday, Great-grandpa!'

Thomas grinned. 'What are you doing out before breakfast, Millie girl? And barefoot too?'

Millie grinned back. It was the same grin as his, Thomas noticed, if you didn't count a thousand freckles instead of grey whiskers.

'My feet feel lighter when they're not closed up in shoes.' Millie held up her pinafore. It had been white, once.

'Mushrooms! They came up last night all over the orchard. I'll probably get the strap,' she added ruefully, looking at the mushroom stains on her pinafore, then looked at him out of the corner of her eye. 'Unless you say something, Great-grandpa! Say I got them for you, special, for your birthday.'

Thomas laughed. 'I might,' he promised. 'Was it you on the lawn looking up at the house a few moments ago?'

'Me? Nope.' Millie put her small hand in his as they began the walk back to the house. The other was occupied with her pinafore and mushrooms. 'I went straight down to the orchard. Did you know there's a wasp's nest there? Grandpa, you will tell them you said I could, won't you?'

'Yes. Yes, I will,' said Thomas absently. So it hadn't been Millie on the lawn. Nor was it the ghost of Pa or Jem, he was sure of that. It had been more than eighty years since he'd seen either of them, but he'd have recognised Jem's ghost. Or Pa's.

'Grandpa?' Millie was looking at him curiously. 'What were you thinking?'

'Do you believe in ghosts, Millie?'

Millie frowned. 'You mean that go "whoo whoo" and frighten you? No. Though Miss Hildegard says the ghost in the cupboard will get me if I don't do my sums.'

Thomas resolved to have a talk with Miss Hildegard.

Millie was looking at him, troubled. 'Grandpa? You're not going to die soon, are you?'

'Me? I hope not,' said Thomas honestly. 'I reckon I've a few more years in me yet.'

'If you died,' said Millie seriously, 'I'd like you to be a ghost. When I take over the farm.'

'When you what?' demanded Thomas.

Millie lifted her chin. It was a gesture Thomas saw in his mirror every day. 'When I take over the farm. I will, you know. Albert doesn't want to be a farmer. He'd rather live in Sydney. So when you die and Grandpa dies and Papa dies, the farm will come to me. And my husband,' she added, 'if I decide to have one. Don't worry, Grandpa,' she added firmly. 'I'll be a good farmer. But ...' she hesitated. 'I'd like sometimes to think your ghost will be there too. Helping me, if things go wrong.'

Thomas felt tears hot in the corners of his eyes. 'I'll be here for you,' he promised. 'If I can.'

'Thank you, Great-grandpa.' It was almost as though the two of them had shaken hands on a contract. Millie looked down at her mushrooms. 'I'd better go or Miss Hildegard will put me in the cupboard with the ghost.'

'She'll what?' roared Thomas. 'You tell Miss Hildegard to see me right now!' he instructed. 'No great-grandchild of mine is going to be locked in a cupboard, ghost or no ghost.'

'I will, Grandpa!' Millie looked gleeful.

Thomas watched her run across the grass, her bare feet leaving footprints in the dew.

Footprints ... Thomas retraced his footsteps and looked around. There were his prints and Millie's. There were no other prints at all.

Ghosts, he thought. Maybe it really was a ghost.

But who? Which ghost of his past would haunt him on his birthday?

Thomas smiled. When you reached ninety, he thought, it could be any one of many.

chapter fourteen

London, 1786

They walked home without the soot, without Jem, without payment either. Master Jack sulked at that. 'Four chimleys, two of 'em double 'uns, and a dead boy for me trouble. Makes the heart sick, it does. And now I've got to buy another boy — that means no work tomorrow either.'

Master Jack took another swig from the bottle in his pocket. ''E's lucky, 'e is,' Jack said savagely, and Tom knew he was referring to Jem. 'Safe in heaven 'e is. No pain in heaven. No soot to rot yer cods an' chest. All the gin that ye can drink in heaven.' He took another swig and wiped tears of self-pity from his eyes.

Tom ignored him. Half of him was numb, the rest furiously thinking. Jem was gone, but their hoard remained. Did he have the courage to try to pawn it by himself? All he knew of London were the streets he'd tramped with Jem. He had no idea how to pawn anything, how to rent a room, or even how to buy a hot potato, much less set up a barrow at Covent Garden.

Where is Covent Garden anyway? thought Tom desperately.

Courage, he thought, and again the image of the red cloak came to his mind, slipping around him, keeping him warm and strong.

I promised Jem, he thought. And now Jem is gone I'll keep the promise.

Jem had found his freedom, the final freedom that his starved and battered body would ever know. And tomorrow, Tom swore to himself, I'll take my freedom too.

* * *

The Bow Street Runners were waiting for them in the room above the cellar, with Lettice wide-eyed and fearful wringing her hands behind them. There were three Runners — two old men with tired faces and a younger one.

Master Jack stared and started to stammer. 'Not me fault. No-one can say it was me fault, chimley just crumbled, that was all.'

'Shut it, old man,' said the younger Runner. 'It's not you we wants.' He grabbed Will and ran his hands about his body. 'Nothin',' he reported.

Tom shrank back as the Runner searched Bertie, then grabbed him too. It took the Runner three seconds to find the handkerchief and coins. The Runner held them up triumphantly. 'Got 'em! Just as the cove said, a guinea piece and threepence and two sixpences. We've got our thief.'

He shook Tom roughly. 'It was yer footprints, ye little fool,' he hissed. 'Sooty footprints across the room, that's how we knew it was a chimney sweep what done it. It had to be one of youse. Come on now, boy. Yer nicked.'

chapter fifteen

Bow Street Court and Newgate Prison, 1786

The court was crowded, onlookers eager for a day's free entertainment. There was little to be had from Tom. The boy pleaded guilty, was bound over for trial at the Old Bailey and sent to Newgate Prison to await it.

They chained the prisoners bound for Newgate together: heavy iron chains about their wrists and ankles, and rusty iron collars about their necks.

Tom stood in the smoky fog outside the Old Bailey. It took all his strength even to stand, with the weight of iron about him. But if he sagged down, the collar about his neck bit cruelly.

He nudged the man chained next to him.

'How long till they take me to trial?' he whispered.

The man looked at him indifferently. He had his own troubles. 'Four months, mebbe.'

'What happens then?'

'What you do?'

'Stole stuff. Money.'

'How much?'

'One pound, two shillings and sixpence.'

'Yer pleaded guilty?'

Tom nodded.

'More fool you. Shoulda kept yer dubber mum'd,' said the man without pity. 'Cove pleads guilty to stealin' more'n a quid they gotta 'ang him. 'Elseways, cove as young as you, they might send 'im to the navy.'

The cold mist dripped down Tom's back, but he hardly felt it. 'How long till they hang me?' he whispered.

The man tried to shrug, but the iron collar stopped him. 'Not long. Took me Bess to see a sprig, younger'n you, seven 'e must've bin, on t' nubbin cheat.[2] Last Michaelmas it were. They 'ad ter put weights about 'is ankles so 'e'd fall quick. Bought Bess a ribbon for 'er 'air, an' an orange too.' He turned away, to look at nothing, remembering perhaps the life he'd lost.

I'm going to die, thought Tom. The knowledge pounded through him. He was going to die like Pa, with the curious gaze of anyone who passed the gallows upon him.

They walked the prisoners to Newgate Prison. The chains weighed more at every step. Tom was stumbling with weariness when they reached the grim granite walls. The high, narrow windows of Newgate Prison stared down at him. Inside was worse.

[2]The nubbin cheat, or chit, was the gallows where people were hanged. Crowds gathered to watch, with fruit, ribbon and sausage sellers.

Had he already died and gone to hell? wondered Tom as he stared around him at the roar of swearing, screams and groans, the stench, the tumbled, crowded huddle of men and women, the thin rags hanging from their bodies, their skin rotting from the cold and damp, covered with ulcers, fleas and bugs.

Yes, it was hell. And after hell, the gallows.

At night Tom slept on bare boards in the men's charity ward, near the corner the prisoners used as a toilet. Despite the smell — or because of it — Tom was safest there from prowling hands and lewd whispers in the night. Each prisoner was supposed to have two blankets; in reality, the strongest amongst them stole what there was. But by now Tom had grown used to cold.

For food he had two three-halfpenny loaves every second day. The bread was supposed to last two days, but Tom learnt quickly to eat it soon. Once the food was in his belly no-one could steal it.

On the next day there was no food at all, and once a week a few shreds of meat. Unlike the more affluent persons on the other side of Newgate, where beds could be hired at sixpence a night, Tom had no money to buy food, bedding or medicine, nor even a shirt to barter for more food.

Men and women mingled during the day in the taphouse, where meals and alcohol could be bought, or in the community rooms or the exercise yard. Sightseers wandered through the prison during the day, holding bunches of herbs or oranges to their noses to block out the stench, laughing as old Mad Maggie danced her naked jig, or poking pins in toothless Charlie to see how the poor mad man neither flinched nor cried.

Other visitors brought food or blankets to family or friends. But there were no visitors for Tom.

There were, however, things to learn in Newgate.

Tom watched as the visitors were jostled, a shoulder bumping them while on the other side a hand slid into their pocket and stole their watch or purse. He watched as prisoners sold their bodies or stole the bread from the dying, and their blankets too.

The first time he picked a pocket he was caught. It didn't worry him. What did he have to lose? There was evidence enough to hang him no matter what else he did.

Long ago, back in the other world when he was loved and clean and had a future, he'd been told that stealing was wrong. But here he was bound for death and hellfire anyway; and at times he thought that neither could be worse than what he'd known.

The visitor with his powdered hair and an orange held to his nose had grabbed Tom's hand when he'd tried to slip it into the silk pocket, and just laughed as he flung the dirty hand away, as though Tom's crime were part of the amusing underworld he'd come to see, and wandered on with his friends, his high heels clicking through the grime.

The next time Tom managed to steal half a crown. It bought him bread for two whole weeks. It would have bought more outside Newgate, but the Newgate keeper had paid well for the privilege of running the prison, and made his fortune at it. Everything, from bread to beds, in Newgate was sold at more than ten times the sum outside.

His blanket was stolen; Tom stole another in turn, from an old man too weak to chase him. The old man died the next day and Tom stole the other blanket from under his body, and the remnants of the man's bread that he'd secreted under his coat to gnaw at with his toothless gums. After that Tom kept his blankets tied around his waist or round his shoulders, even in the exercise yard.

Newgate was a world of its own. And Tom was learning its rules.

I'm a Newgate rat, he thought. And this time the idea gave him a flash of pride.

Rats survived.

chapter sixteen

Newgate Prison, 1787

Tom woke from a nightmare. The Black Man was coming. He'd sucked the life from Jem and now he was coming for Tom too.

Someone gave him a rough kick. 'Bread's be'n given out. Better move y'heels if ye want yours.'

Tom lined up with the others, his blankets wrapped around his shoulders, then clapped the two hard loaves to his chest and sidled through the crowded room, out into the exercise yard.

The stones were cold on his feet; the fog that sifted above the high stone walls was damp and smelt of coal smoke, and it reminded him of the world inside the chimneys.

But at least outside the stench was less; here he could see the yellow haze that meant the sun shone way up above the fog, and remember that it also shone on other places, far from London — places with grass and trees and flowers. Somehow Tom knew it was important to remember that these existed, that there was more in the world than fear and pain.

He nibbled the bread slowly. The fog grew thicker, then lifted as soft rain began to fall. Tom finished the bread and went inside before his rags grew wet.

Where to? Sometimes prisoners left dregs of porter in their mugs in the taproom. If he were quick he might get a swallow, or even two. Or he could linger around the entrance and offer to guide visitors, which might earn him a penny for another loaf of bread. Or . . .

A woman screamed across the common room. Tom paid no attention. Someone was always screaming, fighting, dying or lusting in Newgate. It made no difference to him. He vaguely remembered she had been screaming earlier too.

A hand grabbed his arm. 'You, boy — ye want to earn a penny?'

Tom looked up. It was Bald Sally. No-one knew if Sally was a prisoner or not. She was the prison midwife and seemed to come and go at will.

Tom nodded. Sally's head was scabby between pale tufts of hair. Her face looked like a shrunken apple, with no teeth left at all. But there was still a remnant of kindness in Sally's eyes. Besides, she'd offered him a penny.

'This way, then.' Sally hustled him through the crowd, over to a corner where a woman lay on the dirty floor, her knees up and her skirts hoisted to her waist. The skirts were wet and bloody, and bloody liquid pooled on the floor as well. Tom stared, then looked away.

The woman screamed again. This time the scream went on and on. One of the onlookers laughed.

'None of that,' Sally said to Tom. She pulled him down beside her. 'Ye can't do this with yer eyes shut. Here, wash y'dambles³ in this.'

Tom stared at the bucket on the floor. 'What's in it?'

Sally sighed. 'Toad's vomit and bat's blood, what do ye think? Go on, wash, it's naught but lavender 'n' rosemary 'n' water. Them's the female herbs. If y'going to 'elp me ye need to do it properly.'

Tom washed. The water felt good and smelt even better. 'Can I wash my face as well?'

Sally laughed. 'Well, it'll do 'er naught good nor evil, but if it makes ye happy, go ahead.' She bent down and inspected the woman again. 'Now,' she said to Tom, 'the babe is stuck and can't get out, see, and me dambles be too big to 'elp 'er. But yer dambles might be small enough.'

'What should I do?' whispered Tom, half repulsed, half fascinated. Was this how he had been born, too?

'Pull the babe's 'ead. Y'understand?'

'I understand.' Tom gulped. 'What — what if the baby won't come?'

'Then the babe dies and its ma dies and ye don't get yer penny,' said Sally matter-of-factly.

It was a bit like when he'd rescued Jem, thought Tom in a daze as Sally grasped the screaming, writhing

³Hands.

75

woman to hold her down. 'Soon be over, love,' said Sally to the woman. 'One way or another,' she added.

It was hard to get a grip. Impossible, thought Tom. Then suddenly he had it, his fingers groping till they dug into the soft baby skull. He pulled and felt his fingers slip away. He tried again.

Suddenly the baby slid towards him like a cork out of a bottle. Tom cried out in shock. The mother screamed again, but this scream had as much relief as pain.

Sally shoved Tom roughly out of the way. 'Yer part's done,' she muttered. 'Git outta the way now. I'll see to ye later.'

'But my penny?'

'Ye'll get it! Scram!'

Tom made his way across the room, to a spot where he could watch Sally and make sure she didn't leave without giving him his penny. She was still bending over the mother, the child now in the mother's arms.

I did that, thought Tom in shock. If it hadn't been for me, that baby would never be here at all.

Finally Sally washed her hands again. She said something to the mother, then made her way through the onlookers to Tom. She held the bucket up to him. 'Want ter wash again?'

'Please,' said Tom, dipping his hands in the water. 'Can I have the penny now?' he added.

Sally laughed. 'You've got an 'ead on you, ain't ye? I'll give ye something better than a penny. Come on.'

She made her way to the taproom and made for a

table at the back, occupied already by two men. 'Give yer tuppence to scat,' said Sally, holding out the coins. The men grabbed them and Sally lowered herself into one of the chairs, gesturing to Tom to take the other as she caught the eye of one of the serving women. 'Two of the usual,' she called above the noise.

She turned to Tom. 'Ye did well back there,' she said. 'Done sommat like it before?'

Tom shook his head.

Sally looked at him appraisingly. 'Would ye do it again?'

'For a penny,' said Tom. 'Or tuppence,' he added daringly.

Sally laughed, showing her blackened gums. 'Hark at the lad. I'll feed ye, that's worth more 'n tuppence. What do ye say?'

Tom stared as two bowls of stew were slid onto the table next to them, with two mugs of porter and a round loaf of bread.

'Yes,' he said breathlessly.

Sally tore a lump of the bread and dipped it into the porter to soften it, then began to suck it. Tom took the spoon that was chained to the table so no-one could steal it, and began to eat slowly. The stew was mostly potato, with gobs of pale meat and fat floating in it. Apart from the Christmas potato, it was the first hot food he had eaten for over a year.

Sally dipped more of the bread into the stew, then spooned her lumps of meat into Tom's bowl. 'Can't eat meat with no teeth,' she said cheerfully, taking a swig of porter.

'Mistress Sally.'

'Mmm?' mumbled Sally as she sucked her stew.

'Will the baby be all right? I didn't hurt it, did I?'

'No, lad, ye didn't hurt it. But as for 'er life, well, that babe's bound for the foundling asylum. I wouldn't give yer tuppence for 'er chances there. Most of them babies dies.'

'But her mother's all right, isn't she?'

''Er ma's due to be 'anged,' said Bald Sally flatly, absent-mindedly squashing a louse that fell from her head onto the table. 'They only spared 'er on account of the babe. Now it's born she's for the gallows.' Sally shrugged and gulped her porter.

'Then it was all a waste,' cried Tom, 'if the mother is going to die anyway, and the baby too!'

Bald Sally looked at him sternly. 'Where there's life there's 'ope,' she said. 'If I didn't believe that I couldn't do what I do. Mebbe the babe will live. Mebbe the ma will be pardoned. But once ye give up, lad, yer done fer.'

Tom looked at her doubtfully. Sally looked back at him shrewdly. 'Ye've got courage, lad.'

Tom thought of his courage cloak, and nodded.

Sally grinned. 'Modest like, too. 'Ere, lad, I'll give ye advice that's worth more'n a penny. Three bit's've advice, I'm feelin' generous today. I been seeing 'em come and go from Newgate these last forty year.

'First bit've advice: you're young and small-lookin'.

Play on it, lad. The smaller and more innocent ye look, the better it'll go for ye in the dock.'

'But they'll hang me anyway, won't they?' whispered Tom.

'Mebbe. More like not. Sure, they 'ang ones as young as you, but not if they look properly shamed and small and sweet. So you play small and sweet for all it's worth. Y'understand?'

'I understand,' said Tom slowly, hope blooming.

'You speak nice too,' said Sally approvingly. 'That'll stand ye in good stead. Second bit've advice: what do they 'ave on ye?'

'I stole money and a handkerchief,' said Tom. He didn't mention the other things he and Jem had stolen. 'They found them on me.'

'Then plead guilty. Ye've no chance to prove yer innocence, 'cause y'ain't got none. So like I said, look ashamed and say yer sorry.

'Third bit've advice.' Sally took another slurp of stew. 'An' this'll stand yer in good stead all along yer life, so pay you attention. Ye find a friend and stick to 'em. Take what ye can from the rest o' the world, and bad luck to 'em. But be true to yer friend. Ye'll get further in this world with two o' ye.'

'I don't know anyone in here,' said Tom slowly. 'You said I should play small and young. I'm too small and young to be of use to anyone in here.'

'Ye know me,' said Sally. 'Ye were of use to me.' She stood up. 'The rest is yourn,' she told Tom. 'I best be on me way. But I'll call ye again when I need a hand. Who should I be sending for then?'

'Thomas Appleby,' said Tom.

'Thomas Appleby it is, then.' Sally gave him a rough pat on the shoulder. It was the first touch of kindness Tom had felt for over a year. 'I'll be seeing you, Master Thomas Appleby.'

Sally strode off through the taproom, her high bald head bobbing above the seated murderers and thieves.

Tom never saw her again.

chapter seventeen

The Old Bailey, February 1787

They came for him next morning, and other prisoners too, chaining them together again with the metal collars around their necks and the chains linking each collar to the next, and more chains on their hands. Tom staggered under the weight and wrapped his courage cloak more firmly round his shoulders.

Was this the day that he'd be condemned to die? Sally's words whispered in his ear: 'Play small and sweet. Look sorry for what ye've done.'

It seemed an impossibly long distance to the Old Bailey, the chains clinking, the cold, misty rain dripping down their necks so they were sodden before they'd reached the corner. The chains were too heavy for Tom to even raise his hands to wipe the rain from his eyes, or scratch when a louse ran across his forehead.

I could cry now, thought Tom, and no-one would notice. But he was too frightened for tears. He let the rain run down his face instead and tried to lick the drops. They were the freshest water he'd had since he'd left home.

Finally they reached the court, and stood in the mucky yard till each was called.

'Thomas Appleby!' Tom felt the collar lifted from his neck and the chains taken from his hands. Already his feet felt strangely light without them. He was taken between two constables up the stairs and into the court proper, feeling the stares of the onlookers burning into him.

Would Pa even recognise me as his son? he wondered as he climbed the stairs to the stand. Dressed in rags almost falling off him, thin and prison white except for the dirt, ulcers on his lips and legs, his hair lousy and long as a girl's, wet and matted with filth.

The judge inspected Tom for a moment as the charge was read out.

Small and sweet, thought Tom. I have to play it small and sweet. He hunched his shoulders slightly and tried to look up pitifully.

'Thomas Appleby, what have you to say to the charge?'

'Guilty, sir,' said Tom, as Bald Sally had told him to, in the smallest, most honest voice he had.

The judge peered down at him. 'And do you feel remorse for your crime, Thomas Appleby?'

'Sir?' Tom looked puzzled.

'Say "milord",' hissed the clerk below.

'Milord?' corrected Tom.

'Are you sorry for what you did?' asked the judge impatiently.

'Yes, sir,' said Tom earnestly. Sorry? Of course he was sorry. Sorry he'd been such a fool as to leave sooty footprints. Sorry that he and Jem hadn't got away with it, weren't even now smelling the flowers and eating hot potatoes. But he tried to make his voice sound sincere and ashamed.

'I see.' The judge continued to inspect Tom. 'You are aware, I presume, that if I find you guilty of a theft of one pound, two shillings and threepence halfpenny, as well as the guinea or more that the handkerchief might bring, that I am condemning you to be taken from this court and hanged till you are dead?'

'Yes, sir … milord,' said Tom, feeling desperation pool in the pit of his stomach. It wasn't going to work. No matter how small and shamed he looked, they were going to hang him still!

What had Master Jack said? There is no pain or soot in heaven. Nor in hell either, maybe, thought Tom. He shut his eyes and tried to dream of heaven.

'Which is why I will not be finding you guilty on all of those counts,' continued the judge.

Tom opened his eyes.

'I am aware,' the judge said, looking at Tom steadily, 'that sending you back to Newgate, or to your old haunts, would be trapping you in the life of crime you've known. Instead,' he continued, 'I am dismissing the charge of the theft of the money and finding you

guilty solely on the charge of stealing a handkerchief —
shall we put the value at nineteen shillings and
sixpence? And so, on the lesser charge I sentence you to
seven years' penal servitude and transportation to the
colonies. Constables, you may take the prisoner away.'

Tom was dazed as they led him away. What had the
judge meant? Was he not going to hang then? He had
hoped perhaps to be sent to the navy, to serve there
instead of dying on the gallows ... But transportation?

'Please, sir,' he whispered to one of the constables.
The man turned.

'What is it?'

'What's transportation? Does that mean I'm being
sent to America?'

The man shrugged. 'Don't ask me,' he said.
'America's not taking no more convicts, they say.'

'So what will happen to me? Will I go back to
Newgate?'

The man looked bored. 'Ye'll be taken to the hulks,
that's what, and there to wait His Majesty's pleasure.'

The King again. Tom froze. It had been the King's
pleasure to put Pa in the stocks, it was the King's
pleasure to send him who knows where.

The King had strange pleasures, thought Tom. Even
Master Jack was not as evil as the King.

chapter eighteen

London, February 1787

Tom was chained with the others sentenced in court that day, the metal collar around his neck again, the chains chafing at his wrists and ankles to prevent escape, and loaded onto one of the three open wagons waiting in the prison forecourt.

Each wagon had two guards and a driver, as well as its load of prisoners, men in two of the wagons, and women in the other. Tom peered around the body of the man next to him. They were all much older than him, though none was really old.

'Where are we going?' he asked the man next to him.

The man ignored him, sunk in his own troubles, but one of the others answered: 'Hulks on the Thames, I reckon. If they don't rot afore we gets there.'

'Quiet in the back there!' It was the driver. Then he added, 'None o' you's for the hulks. It's going down to Plymouth, you are. There's a fleet that sets to sail.'

'Where to?' asked someone.

For a moment Tom thought the driver wouldn't answer. Then he said, 'That new place. What's its name again?'

'Botany Bay,' said one of the guards, as the driver jiggled the reins and the horses began to move. The guard laughed shortly. 'Down at the end o' the world, that is. Yer bound for the end o' the world.'

The wagon rumbled through the night and the next day and night too, stopping only for the horses to be changed and for the prisoners to be given a mug of water and a small loaf each. The guards took turns snoozing up front, and complained when it rained.

It was cold, but Tom was used to cold. He was hungry and often thirsty, but he was used to that as well. But now he had fresh air to smell, the scent of soil and grass — he could see the trees and fields, even if the trees were still leafless. There were villages to look at, and stone walls and cottage windows to stare into as the horses plodded past, where families sat at tables or watched the fire, all echoes of the life that he'd once known.

The beauty about him cut Tom like a knife. I'm leaving all this behind, he thought. I'm going to the end of the world.

What would the end of the world be like? Ice maybe, or desert. Tom asked, but no-one knew.

Men worked in the fields as they passed. It was hard to think now that he had once looked down on such men without a trade. Tom would give anything to stand behind a horse and plough or to dig ditches in the quiet air. The men stared at their chains as they passed. They know we are prisoners, thought Tom. We're the scum no-one wants.

It was midday when they reached Plymouth after three days and three nights in the cart, though the tang of the sea had been in their nostrils for two hours or more.

The cart clattered on the cobbles down to the harbourside. Tom gazed out across the water. Ships bobbed on the waves, looking impossibly small.

Which of these am I destined for? Tom wondered. He shivered, only partly from cold. At least in the cart, with the gentle English smells about him, he could dream he was free. There'd be no dreams like that in the dark hold of a ship.

'Whooh there.' The driver pulled on the reins. The cart creaked to a stop. 'Everybody out! Look lively, an' no funny business.'

Tom stumbled from the cart. The chains had chafed his neck and ankles, leaving sores that bled if he moved too much. His legs were cramped and stiff from cold. One by one the prisoners marched along the quay, then down the narrow, slimy steps and into a small boat, with two guards at the oars and another at the tiller.

The boat pulled away from the quay. Suddenly Tom knew with dreadful clarity that he'd never set foot again on English ground. The growing distance between himself and land was just the start of their permanent separation.

They were passing the first of the ships now. Tom craned to see each one as they passed, frighteningly small vessels to carry them across the world. One was called the *Friendship* and he felt a pang of grief, remembering Jem. He half hoped this ship would be his destination. But the guards rowed past it, to the *Scarborough* instead.

The rowing boat bumped against the side of the *Scarborough*, near a damp rope ladder hanging down over the side of the ship. The convicts climbed the ladder one by one. Tom gripped the wet rope and hauled himself upwards. The ladder swung with every step, and the weight of the chains made the swinging worse. If the man in front or behind fell he'd be drowned too, thought Tom — dragged down into the waves by the weight of iron. But no-one fell.

It felt strange to stand on the rocking deck. A guard unlocked each of their chains in turn. Tom looked at the blue and bloody bruises on his wrists and ankles where the chains had rested, then looked away.

'Strip!' muttered the guard. Tom stared. 'I said strip! All of yez!' the man ordered more loudly.

Tom pulled his ragged shirt over his head, feeling the damp wind bite into his bare flesh, and then removed his tattered breeches. Now the prisoners were all naked, standing in the cold sea wind for everyone to stare at. Two by two they clambered into half-barrels full of seawater, and were given fatty cakes of carbolic soap to wash away the dirt and vermin while their hair was clipped close to their heads to remove the lice.

Tom looked at the soapy scum on the water. There's chimney soot in there, he thought, and Newgate stench. At least I'm free of those, no matter what comes next.

Tom left the water reluctantly. At least the barrel hid his skinny, naked limbs and the dark bruises. It was even colder standing wet on the deck. There were no towels. Instead Tom was lined up with the other convicts, all dripping, all naked and bald, and handed coarse trousers, two shirts, a jacket and stockings, a cap and a pair of shoes — all far better than the rags Tom had worn for the past year, and clean too. He put them on gladly, feeling their crispness and cleanliness against his skin.

A clanging sound warned him. The guards hauled chains from a rusty pile on the deck, a cuff of rusty metal for each ankle, with a thick chain in between, long enough to let you walk but not to run or move quickly.

The chains were designed for a man, not a boy. But they were no worse than the chains Tom was used to.

'Move!' yelled the guard. The prisoners shuffled forward again, their chains clanging and sliding on the damp wood, towards a dark hole in the deck.

Tom stared at the hole. Not down there, he thought. It's like the chimneys. Please don't let us go down there.

But, one by one, the prisoners turned to clamber down the ladder into the hole. Tom took a final breath of brisk salt air, a final look at the seagulls soaring across the blue.

It was to be his last glimpse of the sky for months.

Down, down, down ... with every step his chains dangled and weighed at his ankles. Tom stared into the gloom. There were no portholes, and no lanterns or candles either. It was impossible to see.

Tom stepped off the ladder and onto the damp floor. The blackness was impenetrable after the bright sunlight up on deck. Beside him the men had to bend almost double in the confined space. At least he could stand upright.

It smelt of tar and sweat and privies. And it was full of people. The guard yelled down into the gloom. 'Find yerselves a berth. Look lively now!' He began to pull up the ladder.

Tom tried to see where to go. His eyes were adjusting to the gloom now. He could just make out two rows of wooden slatted sleeping berths one above each other, each about six feet square.

A face leered out from one of the nearby berths as the hatch shut above them, cutting off the last of the light. 'Four to a berth! Here, young 'un, you go up with Sailor Sam. There's still space there.'

Tom went where he was shoved. There was no other choice in the sudden darkness. A leathery hand reached down and pulled him up onto one of the upper berths. Tom tried to sit, and bumped his head on the ceiling. He slithered down onto his stomach instead.

It was impossible to see his companion, but the hand had been calloused. 'And who do you be?' demanded a voice.

It was an old man's voice, hoarse and unsteady. The breath stank like a privy.

'Thomas Appleby. Tom.'

The hand grasped his again. 'Well, Tom, welcome aboard.' The throaty voice seemed genuinely friendly, despite the smell. 'They call me Sam.'

'What is your real name then?' asked Tom.

'Sam!' The old voice cackled as though it was a hilarious joke. 'Ye got yer bundle? Good lad, then. Best to tie it to yer berth. No, let Sam do it for ye. Sam's sailed the seven seas, man and boy. Sam'll see ye right on board.'

'Which seven seas were they?' Tom couldn't care less where the old sailor had gone. But the thought of being alone in this confusion of dark and stench and noise terrified him. Talking to anyone — even an old sailor who stank of bad teeth and poor digestion — was better than nothing.

'North Sea, Mediterranean Sea, Sargasso Sea, Caribbean Sea, Labrador Sea ...'

Tom counted. 'That's only five seas,' he objected.

The cackle came again. 'There'll be seven and more by the time we've finished this journey, matey.'

'How long were you a sailor?' Talking kept the darkness at bay.

'Weren't a sailor at all,' said Sam. 'They just calls me that. Goes with Sam, I reckon. 'Sides, I know all about the sea, more'n any of this lot 'ere. I were a marine, I were. Fought in the war in the Americas.'

Tom nodded in the darkness. He didn't need to ask how Sam had come from being a marine to a convict.

91

There had been plenty like Sam in Newgate. There had been few jobs once the men had been released from the army and the navy after the war with America. Many had chosen theft instead of starvation.

'Did you come from Newgate too?'

Tom felt rather than saw Sam shake his head. 'Most comes from the prison ships on the Thames. Ye'll be one of the last boatloads to come aboard, I reckon.'

'Why do you think that?'

''Cause up to a week ago they 'ad us workin' on the docks, movin' rocks to make the breakwater or mannin' the hand dredge to deepen the harbour. But now they've got us locked up tighter than a rat's behind. Any tide now we're off to Botany Bay, an' a good thing too.' Sam spat down into the darkness. ''Ad enough o' land, I have. Nothin' good 'as come of it since I been ashore.'

'Who else sleeps on this berth?' Already the soft rocking of the ship made Tom feel queasy, and strangely sleepy too.

'Black Bob and John the Tooth,' said Sam. 'They be over in the corner, playing dice.'

'But it's too dark to see!'

Again Tom felt rather than saw the shrug. 'You can feel the dice. No need to see 'em. Played dice meself in darkness many a time. That were when we was becalmed off the Carolina coast. Strange, that were ...'

Tom lay back to listen, using his bundle as a pillow. His stomach seemed easier lying down and, besides, he'd had little sleep the last few days in the cart. He dozed off to the soft cackle of Sam's voice. 'Grey sky and grey water, the clouds just sat there but not a drop did we have to drink. Over 'alf the crew we lost that month alone.'

It was the first of hundreds of stories Tom was to hear, crammed up with Sam on the berth in the darkness; stories of shipwrecks and mermaids and waves that were higher than fifty ships.

At first Tom thought that they were lies. No man could have lived through them all, especially Sailor Sam, who could hardly be over fifty or he wouldn't have been chosen to go to the colonies. But the years of starvation at sea (and worse in an American prison), the scurvy and the imprisonment had aged Sam. With his teeth all gone he sounded a hundred years old, and in daylight looked seventy or more.

But Sam's stories kept the boredom away in the endless hours below deck, when the only air or light came through the hatch, and even that vanished in bad weather.

And the stories were true, or mostly. If they hadn't happened to Sam, they had to someone he'd known. It seemed there was a lot of time for stories at sea. Some were fantastic, like the sea monster washed up on the Yankee beach, sixty feet from top to tail. But others told the boy about the world. Sam had a memory for every word he'd heard, and a gift for storytelling too. And Tom had nothing to do in the damp, smelly darkness but listen.

It seemed that voyaging at sea was a dangerous matter, even if you weren't at war with the French or the Americans. Over a third of sailors died at sea, from scurvy,[4] starvation, thirst, dysentery or lost limbs or eyes. And Lieutenant James Cook[5] was the only English captain who had ventured as far as Botany Bay.

'Botany Bay,' said Sam, in the midst of another tale. 'Aye, that's where we're 'eaded, afore the Frenchies beat us to it and take the land. Ye mark my words, we'll be at war with they Frenchies again afore too long.' Sam seemed enthusiastic even though he would not be there to see it.

'What's Botany Bay like?'

Sam scratched his head, then kept scratching as he dislodged a scab from between what was left of his hair. 'Ah, it's a grand place, they say.'

'Really!' Tom felt a thread of hope. 'Who says?'

'The captain that went there, oh, nigh on twenty years ago it were now, Lieutenant Cook. I sailed with Tin Hand Jim, an' he sailed with Cook. Tin Hand Jim, 'e saw it all.'

[4]This was caused by a lack of vitamin C from fresh fruit and vegetables, but in Tom's day it was thought that it might be caused by too much salted meat or too much time at sea. Good captains like Cook and Phillip, however, knew that fresh food helped ward off scurvy, even if they didn't know about vitamin C, and went to enormous efforts to make sure all on their ships had as much fresh fruit and vegetables as possible.

[5]James Cook was captain of the ship, but his naval rank was lieutenant.

'What did he see?' asked Tom impatiently. 'Are there big towns there? And farms?'

Sam cackled. 'Farms? Not on your nelly, matey. There are no farms, nor cities neither! Only black heathens — big, tall Indians naked as the day they were born, with spears and long fur cloaks and —'

'You said the Indians were naked,' interrupted Tom.

'Naked under their cloaks, boy. Don't interrupt or I'll tell ye no further.'

Tom grinned in the darkness. There was no chance of Sam stopping his stories. He even talked in his sleep, and screamed sometimes, which was why no-one else had wanted to share the berth with him. But Sam never told the stories behind his nightmares, or at least, not to Tom.

'Strange monsters there are, too, rabbits more'n six foot high that jump on their hind legs.'

'Are you sure?' demanded Tom.

'Sure as sure! Didn't Tin Jim tell me it? An' fish in the sea and trees all full of fruit. We'll 'ave a grand time there, boy. A grand time.' And Sam's voice was full of hope, for himself as well as Tom.

Darkness, stench and crowding — but it was better than Newgate, and better than the cellar too. At least here there was no work to tear your bones, no soot to wear in every crevice of you.

The food was far better as well — two slices of bread for breakfast, pease soup with fresh vegetables for dinner, and even fresh meat in the soup sometimes.

It had been a year since Tom had tasted fresh meat or vegetables, apart from the potatoes on Christmas Day and the meal he had shared with Bald Sally. Oatmeal porridge for supper, a mug of beer once a week, and even if the bread was stale and even green and there were weevils in the porridge, well, as Sam said, a bit o' weevil did no-one any harm. And at least the food was regular and even hot, and shared out proper like, in pannikins, so each man got his feed.

There were two buckets for a privy that all the prisoners shared, hauled upwards by the guard. There was an infirmary, with a surgeon who inspected each of the convicts. Tom's ulcers were painted and gradually healed.

The visit to the surgeon was the only time in the three weeks before the ship sailed that Tom was allowed up on deck. Orders forbade convicts on the deck until the ship was out of sight of land, in case they mutinied, as some had done before, and sailed off with the ship. But those convicts had come to a bad end, said Sam — they'd all been taken or eaten by savages far away.

Tom peered back at the shore. Grey and misty now in the constant winter rain. The seagulls shrieked overhead, hoping for slops. This would be the last time he'd see England for seven years.

Forever, said a whisper in his brain. Goodbye to Pa, to Jem. You are saying goodbye forever.

chapter nineteen

Murruroo, Australia,
15 April 1868

Thomas Appleby sat in his chair on the verandah overlooking the lawn and digested his breakfast: stewed peaches, porridge, kidneys and bacon, some of Millie's mushrooms fried in butter by the cook, a slice of toast with marmalade from their own orange trees, three good strong cups of tea.

It was a breakfast that a man could do some work on, but these days Thomas Appleby needed time to let it settle.

Fancy thinking he had seen a ghost this morning! Well, at his age it wouldn't be surprising if his eyes were no longer clear, thought Thomas morosely.

But his eyesight wasn't as bad as that, surely. He could see the willow trees along the riverbank, where once the red gums grew; they had cut those gums for fence posts. He could see the river and the hills.

The land was his, as far as the eye could see.

In truth, the hills blocked the eye from seeing very far at all, but still, 4000 acres was a goodly property. Four thousand acres, five children living — Joshua, Marcus and the girls — twenty-seven grandchildren, forty-three great-grandchildren ... give me time, Thomas thought contentedly, and I'll have filled up half of Australia.

They called it Australia now, not New Holland any more, to wipe away the shame of the country's convict past. My past, too, thought Thomas Appleby, and smiled. Who alive remembered the convict boy who'd stared at the blank green face of Australia and wrapped the courage cloak around himself and swore that he'd survive?

Perhaps, thought Thomas, the ghost on the lawn was me as a boy, all those years ago, come to haunt me again now.

But no, the ghost hadn't worn convict garb. And, besides, that boy had been transformed. And in his place sat Thomas Appleby — grazier, magistrate — his convict past carefully forgotten. One of Martha's boys was even talking of going back to England to Oxford University to study, like the gentleman he was.

No, it would not be a good thing for a gentleman at Oxford to own up to an ex-convict great-grandfather. How could the scholars in their robes ever understand the way it had been for a small boy trapped in London's slums?

Some things were best forgotten; just as the floods swept the river clean, time swept the pain of it away.

Will there ever come a day, thought Thomas, when there'll be no shame in looking back? It was an amazing thing we did back then, crossing four oceans in our tiny ships, to a place only one English captain had ever sailed to before, and settling an unknown land. But no-one wants to remember those days now.

chapter twenty

The *Scarborough*, May 1787

On the evening of May 12th, Captain Phillip ordered the fleet to weigh anchor and set sail for the new land.

Nothing happened: the sailors were on strike. The owners of the ships hadn't paid them for seven months and they refused to sail until they got their money.

Finally, at three in the morning on the next day, Tom felt the strange vibration as the wind filled the sails and the anchor was lifted. The ship was no longer rocking back and forth, tossed by the English waves. Instead, as the wind grew stronger in the grey dawn light, the ships headed out to sea.

Of the eleven ships that were to be known as the First Fleet, two were naval warships — the *Sirius*, which also carried Captain Phillip, and the *Supply*. The other ships were converted merchant ships, hired by the government for the voyage: three store ships and six transports, with 736 convicts aboard. There were about 1450 people in all — officers, surgeons, sailors, marines and their families, as well as the convicts.

Most of the convicts were aged between twenty and thirty-five; many were farm labourers convicted of minor theft, highway robbery or theft of sheep or cattle. There was one gardener, one fisherman, five shoemakers, two brickmakers; there were also ivory turners, glove makers, oyster sellers and milliners — jobs for which there would be little use in Botany Bay.

Most of the women had been domestic servants. There were no convicted murderers, no rapists. Tom was the second youngest of all the convicts, the doctor told him, and the youngest on their ship, and Sam one of the oldest, though there were a few still older than he.

By afternoon of the first day at sea the convicts were allowed on deck for air and exercise, lugging their chains in an endless shuffle around the deck. It was bliss to stand again in the fresh air, to stretch cramped limbs even though the tiny deck was crowded. Tom edged his way to the rail and gazed about him.

No, they were not totally out of sight of land. There in the misty distance behind him was a thicker mist that held his past — Pa, Jem, Master Jack, the fields where he'd hunted mushrooms only eighteen months before, the hedges where he'd picked cobnuts and chewed the bitter haws.

Would there be haws or cobs in Botany Bay? Of course there would, he thought uncertainly. It was country, wasn't it? You always found cobs and haws out in the country.

But there would be no chimneys, at any rate, or none at least till he was too old to climb them. Whatever Botany Bay held for him, thought Tom, it wasn't chimneys.

The convicts were allowed out only on the lower deck. The officers, marines, guards and their families used the upper deck. Between the two decks was a barricade about three feet high, armed with pointed iron prongs. Tom looked at the people on the upper deck curiously: two women in wide bonnets, staring back towards the vanished land; marines in their bright uniforms.

And a boy. A boy his age, or maybe a year older, dressed like he had been only eighteen months ago: good breeches, boots and stockings, a cap upon his head. And no chains, thought Tom. It had been so long since he had been able to move without the constant weight and chafing of his chains.

The boy must have felt Tom looking. He turned and caught Tom's eye, then hurriedly turned away.

'All below!' bellowed one of the guards. 'And I mean now!'

The horde of convicts limped obediently down the hatch once more.

chapter twenty-one

At sea, 1787

The sunlight streamed down upon the fleet; the wind filled their sails. Each day was spent up on deck. It was the most sunlight Tom had known for more than a year, with better air and better food and, if not kindness, at least less brutality than he'd known before.

'Ah, a fair wind behind us,' said Sam, standing next to him on the deck.

Tom wasn't sure he even liked Sam much, or that Sam liked him. But Sally had said he needed a friend, and it was true that having a friend, even one like Sam, made life easier for them both. Sam kept the darkness from closing in, and gave Tom the bits in his stew that were too tough for his toothless gums to chew. In turn, Tom listened to Sam's stories, even the ones he'd heard a dozen times before, and stole another blanket for him.

It was easy for Tom to sneak about in the darkness of the hold. He was smaller by far than anyone else there and, moreover, his year in the cellar and the chimneys had trained him well in creeping about small places in the dark. He could even keep his chains silent now as he snuck along. It was a pity, he thought, that there wasn't anything worthwhile to steal.

Sam wasn't Jem, but Sam was better than facing the darkness with no friend at his side.

In three weeks the fleet dropped anchor in the harbour at Santa Cruz on the island of Tenerife. The convicts were imprisoned in the darkness below deck for a week while the fleet loaded fresh meat and onions and pumpkins and water.

The meat was stringy and dark, but the servings were generous while they were in harbour, and the stews full of fresh vegetables too. Captain Phillip was making sure his charges were as healthy and well fed as possible for the coming voyage.

Then another week to the Cape Verde Islands, where the wind lashing the ship was too strong for them to land and sped them into the Atlantic and onwards to South America.

On deck, the wide blue of sky and sea around them, Tom watched as Sam dipped his fingers in the water trough and outlined a rough map on the deck.

'We wuz 'ere, see, up in England. We went down the coast of Africa and now we 'ead to 'ere, across the Atlantic Ocean.'

Tom studied the map, puzzled. 'But why do we go all the way to South America if Botany Bay is way past Cape Town? Shouldn't we just keep going down along the coast of Africa?'

Sam cackled his toothless laugh. 'No, lad, thou's not thinking like a sailor. A sailor knows we 'ave ter 'ave the wind. If we drop down to Rio we pick up the Westerlies. They'll take us straight to Botany Bay like a pigeon dropping through the sky.'

Tom stared at the map. It was already drying on the deck. It was hotter now, too hot for a jacket or stockings. 'Is that what Botany Bay looks like?' he asked. The land Sam had sketched looked neat and round.

Sam shook his head. 'Nobbut knows what the whole land is like, seeing as nobbut's sailed around it. That's just me drawing, see? No, it's an unknown land right enough.'

Tom shivered, but there was excitement too. He should feel scared. He *did* feel scared. But at night he had his courage cloak to wrap around him. And unknown as the new land was, at least it had possibilities for good. There had been none at all in his previous changes of fortune.

Tom glanced over the wood and iron barrier that separated the convicts from the passengers, automatically looking for the boy. There was no sign of him, though the woman Tom had decided must be his mother stood at the rail, staring out, her shawl around her although the day was hot. Suddenly she called, 'Rob! Rob, come here!'

The boy's head appeared from the upper hatchway. 'Mama?'

'Robbie, look!' She pointed out at sea. Tom craned to look as well. Something soared high into the air, then crashed down into the spray; there was another, and another still.

'Porpoises,' remarked Sam, following his gaze. 'They means good luck and a smooth crossing.'

'Really?' asked Tom, one eye still on the other boy.

Sam nodded. 'So they say.' He spat noisily on the deck.

The boy and his mother were still talking beside the rail. Neither even glanced towards the convicts. Tom shrugged and turned to listen to another of Sam's tales.

But now he knew that the boy's name was Rob.

chapter twenty-two

At sea, 1787

Suddenly the heat seemed to burst about them. The bilge water at the bottom of the ship seeped upwards, as though drawn by the hot sun, bringing with it an almost unbearable stench of privies, dead rats and vomit.

Even the guards stood back now when the hatch was opened. Tom felt his lungs begin to rot, and his eyes streamed with pain and irritation. His skin burnt with the bites of fleas and bugs and every tiny beast that lived on human flesh.

When the sea was rough the bilge water sloshed up over the lower berths. But the other two inmates of Tom and Sam's berth were sturdy, even if Sam and Tom were not, and fought off any takers for their position above the worst of the filth.

Sam had the runs. Tom waded through the filth to fetch the privy bucket as often as he could. So many had the runs now. The buckets were full, or guarded jealously by those stronger and older than Tom. Sam's clothes were fouled, and the floor about them too, though at least the bilge water washed the worst of it away.

There were storms now that shook the ship and heaved it from side to side. The food grew foul and the water worse, but they drank it anyway, their bodies craving moisture.

Tom got the runs as well.

Then one morning he woke to find the crash of waves had stopped. The wind had dropped too. The shuddering forward motion of the ship had ceased. Instead they swayed languidly from side to side.

Sam muttered something as he lay next to Tom on the bed. Tom craned closer to listen amid the noise of the others and the creaking of the hold. 'Doldrums, boy,' said Sam weakly. His breath stank even worse now, and there was a new sour–sweet smell to it as well. 'We're in the doldrums now.'

'What are the doldrums?' asked Tom. Somehow, he thought, if Sam keeps talking he'll stay alive.

'No wind, no currents. Knew a ship once that wandered three years in the doldrums, waiting for a wind to blow it free,' whispered Sam. 'The sailors ate the rats, they ate the sails, they started to eat each other.'

'And then what happened?' demanded Tom.

But Sam had fallen into a muttering sleep.

The air felt hot and still, too thick it seemed for ships to journey through it. Water was scarce and rationed to three pints per man per day. Food was scarce too.

Day by day dragged by. At least now that the storms had moved on the convicts could go up on deck every day. At the end of the second week Tom helped Sam up the hatchway at morning exercise and saw him settled weakly against the rail, then breathed deeply, as though if he took in enough air now he needn't breathe down below until the fresh air tomorrow. His feet were stained with the sludge of the bilges. His eyes, he knew, must be red from the foul air below and his skin had erupted in a million bites from lice and fleas and cockroaches. But at least up here there was sunlight and the sharp salt smell of the ocean.

He looked over at the other deck. Rob was there most days. He seemed a strange boy, happy to be alone, or as alone as you could be aboard a ship, sometimes reading but mostly sketching on a white-paged pad. Tom wondered what there was to sketch on board. Even the sea birds had vanished. The sky was empty, without bird or cloud.

But today there was no sign of Rob, or of his mother. The deck was empty. Then slowly it began to fill again, till all the marines were assembled and many of the crew were too, and the captain, a Bible in his hand.

What was going on? Was it a funeral? There had been several since the ship had left. There was still no sign of Rob, nor of his mother.

A drum rolled. A sudden certainty filled Tom's heart. Three men and a boy stepped somberly up the hatch then across the deck, bearing a coffin on their shoulders.

The boy was Rob.

Tom watched as the captain spoke, too far away for Tom to catch his words. The coffin slid down into the ocean. It bobbed there for a second, then sank.

'Got 'er weighted down,' muttered Sam. He staggered up to stand next to Tom. 'Cap'n don't want a coffin followin' us at sea. Bad luck if a coffin floats.'

'Do you know who it was?' asked Tom, though in his heart he already knew.

'Be one of the marine's wives. Not an officer's — officer's can't bring their families with 'em. Sergeant's wife, p'raps. That old cove carryin' the coffin had a sergeant's stripes.'

One of the convicts passing on a continuous shuffle around the tiny deck heard him and stopped his endless walk. 'Sergeant Stanley's wife, it were. Baby came too early, 'cause she had the flux, an' it killed her.'

Sam coughed. 'Flux? Same as me then, boy. But I won't die,' he added, seeing Tom's look. 'Old sailors are pickled in seawater. If the sea don't get me nothing will. Don't ye worry, lad. We'll get the winds soon, ye'll see. This is a lucky ship. I feels it in my water.'

The funeral party was breaking up. Soon only the sergeant and the boy were standing at the rail, watching where the coffin had disappeared. The sergeant looked too old to be Rob's father — far older than Tom's Pa had been and much older than his wife had been. But he hugged the boy's shoulders roughly, as a father might, then went to speak with the captain. The boy, Rob, stood there alone.

Tom watched him. Suddenly Rob turned and met his eyes. It was almost as though he had known Tom was watching all along, had seen the funeral and the coffin disappear.

Tom stood too embarrassed to speak or move. He hadn't felt this helpless since Pa was in the stocks.

Courage, he thought. I swore I'd act with courage.

He thrust the embarrassment away. He was a convict, the other a marine's son. But despite this he raised his chin and mouthed, 'I'm sorry.'

There was no way the other could hear him above the noise of the dragging chains on the convicts being punished for fighting, the wind and flapping sails. But perhaps Rob understood. He nodded once, his face expressionless, then turned and went below.

chapter twenty-three

At sea, 1787

Sam was right. In three days the high winds blew again, the south-east trades. The small ships sped along. Another week of heat and thirst and then they hit Rio.

The convicts were imprisoned below again.

They were to stay in darkness the whole month they were in Rio harbour, their only fresh air that which blew through the hatch, smelling of strange trees and spices. The bilges were pumped out, the foul water further polluting Rio's harbour but making the space below decks almost tolerable.

The unrelieved darkness was hard to bear, but the food was extraordinarily good: fresh beef, more than Tom had ever eaten in one day, and ten oranges a day too, small ones with blood-red flesh — Tom caught a glimpse of their colour when the hatch was opened — and giant oranges with yellow skins.

Tom had only eaten oranges before at Christmas, and then only one that Pa bought as a treat. He had sucked the juice before he ate the flesh, then kept the dried peel to eat months later, still smelling the bitterness that spoke of far-off lands and sun.

There were so many oranges now there was no reason to eat them slowly, though Tom saved their skins to eat later on. Sam shook his head at the oranges. 'Make me gums sting something awful, lad. You eat my share.'

Sam ate the other fruit though, soft squishy things called guavas that Tom had never seen before, and nor had any of the other men inside the hold; fruits that smelt of flowers, confusing smells that showed how far they'd come from all they'd known.

Even the harbour sounded foreign. Tom could hear the natives yelling as their canoes bumped the side of the *Scarborough*, selling their melons and pumelos, persimmons, tangerines and guavas, pumpkins and oranges sweet and firm and smelling of sunlight and lands that Tom would never see, despite sitting in their harbours in the crowded ship.

The next stop would be Cape Town — the final port before the long stretch across the whole of the Indian Ocean, through the Southern Ocean and into the Pacific to Botany Bay.

It was again a quick crossing to Cape Town, not much more than a month. Sam was recovering, though very weak. Tom rarely saw Rob these days. He seemed to avoid the deck when the convicts were above.

The marines were often drunk now, with the new supplies of cheap alcohol they'd bought in Rio. Several times marines were strapped to the mast on deck and flogged for fights or drunkenness. The convicts were kept below during the floggings, but the sound was unmistakable — lash, lash, lash — so you counted them in your mind … ten, fifty, two hundred even one time, and then the slump as the bleeding body was unstrapped and fell to the deck, the swish as it was dragged away, and the sound of water splashing to wash the blood away.

The convicts were lashed, too, for any disobedience, but never so many lashes as the marines. The convicts were the scum of the earth, thought Tom bitterly. No-one expected good behaviour from a convict.

Once the ship anchored at Cape Town the prisoners were again confined below, but it was easier this time. The weather was cooler than it had been in Rio and, besides, Captain Phillip was determined to make his charges as healthy as possible before the six-and-a-half thousand mile sweep before them.

It was an extraordinary distance for a fleet like his to travel, following a scarcely known route and not just with sailors, but with women and men he needed to keep healthy so they could work when they reached their final port.

So the ships were cleaned, fires lit between decks to kill off fleas and lice, then every surface scrubbed with tar oil, the bilges were pumped out again — everything that could be done to clean the ship of contagion and filth before the last leg of their journey was undertaken before they set sail.

Even better, from Tom's point of view, was the food.

Once more, now they were in harbour, there were as many vegetables and fruits as the convicts could eat — more and more again, served every day, and soft fresh bread and fresh meat, too.

Sam's toothless mouth could manage the bread, but his gums were too tender for the meat or fruits, and his hands trembled too much to even tear them into small portions he could swallow.

The prisoners weren't allowed knives to cut their food, or even spoons — spoons could be beaten flat and sharpened to be used like knives and, besides, spoons cost money. Finally Tom chewed Sam's meat for him and crushed the fruits so that their juices ran into Sam's pannikin for him to drink.

Sam's runs had stopped after Rio, and his guts no longer heaved. He didn't even have the hoarse cough of so many of the prisoners, and there'd been no cases of typhus aboard their ship, though other ships hadn't been so lucky. But Sam was weaker every day, despite the mild weather.

The ship sank deep into the harbour, loaded with new supplies. The convict berths were crushed even closer together as room was made for sheep, cows, horses, hens and pigs, more than 500 official animals to be taken to the new colony, plus 'unofficial' animals bought by the officers and marines for their own use once they'd landed.

The weather grew hot with the approach of summer. The sheep bleated pitifully in the heat below decks, while the sailors made constant trips to keep them fed and watered.

At least the stink is different, thought Tom as he listened to the terrified bleating of the sheep beyond the narrow partition that separated the animals from the convicts. It was an almost pleasant smell, reminding him of the fields at home where he'd gone mushrooming.

Would there be fields at Botany Bay? Not fields as such, of course. The savage Indians there didn't have any fences. But maybe there'd be mushrooms in the grass.

Seven years — that was most of his life so far. But he'd be only sixteen when he'd done his sentence. Realising this, for the first time Tom felt a breath of hope, bred by the fresh food and the familiar smell of sheep.

The ships stayed a month at Cape Town, then sailed again.

Now, finally, the convicts were allowed up on deck. Tom clambered up the ladder eagerly. Fresh air! But the light was far too bright, and the sky seemed too high.

Tom turned and helped haul Sam up the ladder too. Sam was so weak now he couldn't climb himself, and so light that even Tom could lift him. But the sunlight will do Sam good, thought Tom stubbornly. He'll get better now he can have sunlight.

It was strange to be able to stand upright on the deck again, after so many days cramped down below. Sam staggered up the hatch beside Tom, most of his weight resting on the boy's shoulders.

'Soon be better again,' he wheezed. 'Just need the salt air in me lungs, ye'll see.'

Tom left him lying against the rail and staggered around the deck with the men, each willing their legs to work again after so long spent crouched or lying. Tom stretched his arms above his head and wondered what it would be like to be a bird, to fly above it all. To fly wherever he willed.

Where would I fly, he wondered, if I could choose? Only to the past, and even a bird can't fly there.

Back to England? No, not England. There was nothing for him there and despite the fact he'd sailed halfway around the world, he'd seen none of it.

To Botany Bay? Was it really as good as Sam said? What would it be like to go to Botany Bay as a free man ... or as a bird ...

Tom glanced over the rail and there was Rob. He had another book in his hands. Pa had taught Tom to read — a printer had to know the words before he could set up the type. But it was nearly two years now since Tom had touched a book. He wondered if he had forgotten what to do with one.

As Tom watched, Rob slipped the book carefully into the pocket of his jacket. He then looked straight at Tom, but once again immediately looked away.

Convict scum, thought Tom. That's what I am. But two years ago I was as good as you. Better, for my pa had a trade and yours is just a marine.

It was the last time Tom would see the sky for thirteen days.

chapter twenty-four

Murruroo, Australia, 15 April 1868

Thomas Appleby sat on the verandah and tried to look as though he were listening to Miss Hildegard, instead of watching for the ghost.

'The girl is disobedient,' said Miss Hildegard firmly, her Prussian accent even stronger now that she was angry. She had come to Australia during the gold rushes with her parents, nearly twenty years ago. But the accent still lingered.

'She will not wear her boots — her good button boots! Today she climbed out her window and down the loquat tree! Always I tell her, "You must be a lady, Millicent. No-one will wish to marry a girl who is not a lady, no matter how important her papa is" — and her great-grandpapa too,' she added hurriedly. 'Such a great family she comes from! But she will not listen. Never is she listening.'

'Miss Hildegard,' said Thomas firmly. 'My great-granddaughter is not to be punished if she forgets to wear her boots. Feet need to breathe sometimes. And she is never — do you understand? — never to be locked in a cupboard, or anywhere at all, no matter what she does!'

'But if she disobeys ...' began Miss Hildegard.

'Send her to me,' said Thomas. 'I will deal with her.'

Miss Hildegard gave him an uncertain look. But no-one argued with Thomas Appleby. She bobbed a curtsey instead. 'Yes, Mr Appleby. I will remember.'

'See that you do,' said Thomas.

He felt a bit guilty after she had left — Miss Hildegard did a good enough job. But he wasn't having a child of his blood locked in darkness.

chapter twenty-five

Cape of Good Hope, 1787–88

The change came suddenly: just the normal rock and sway of the ship that night, a little rougher than most, then all at once the ship shuddered and seemed to climb — higher, higher, impossibly high, then higher still.

The hold sloped like it had suddenly become a hill. Men fell from their berths, swearing as their heavy chains jarred against their limbs. The sheep cried from their prison beyond. Only the hens were silent, still asleep in the dense darkness, clasping their perches hard, perhaps, so they wouldn't fall off.

'Sam! What's happening?' Tom clung to the wooden floor of their berth with one hand and onto Sam with the other. The old man didn't have the strength to hold on himself, not with the weight of his chains on his skinny flesh and bones.

Sam raised his head. 'What do ye think — that we've gone and climbed a mountain? The ship's heading up a wave, lad!'

'But waves aren't as big as this!'

For a second the ship hung level as it reached the

wave top, then plunged back down again. The men who had clambered back on the berths were flung off again. Someone screamed, the eerie noise going on and on.

'Are we going to sink?' yelled Tom, above the noise.

'Tie me to the berth, matey!'

'But if we're going to sink ...'

'Don't be a fool! We ain't gonna sink. Not from this, at any rate. It's just the Cape. 'Tis always bad round the Cape, they say,' said Sam, forgetting he'd claimed to have sailed every sea there was. 'Now tie me on!'

Tom fumbled with the blankets as the ship began to climb again. He'd just tied the first knot when the ship plunged down once more.

Already the hold smelt of vomit and urine as men lost control in fear. The sheep squealed; even the ship itself groaned as though every plank of wood was pained.

Tom pulled the last knot tight about Sam, who was now held firm by both blankets.

'Tie yerself on too,' muttered Sam.

It was harder tying himself fast, but Tom managed it. The other men on their berth saw what he was doing and copied him. The idea spread from berth to berth.

Up again ... Once more the ship climbed impossibly high. Tom held himself tense, waiting for the fall. If the ship sank they'd be imprisoned here, unable to get free as the ship fell through the cold black water. And even if they did manage to break out of the hold, what then? Who on the whole ship knew how to swim? And who could swim in seas like these?

'Did I ever tell ye of Mad Mike?' muttered Sam in Tom's ear.

Tom shook his head. 'No.' His hands were gripping the sides of the bunk so hard they hurt. It was stupid, he knew. If the waves swamped the ship he'd drown, no matter how hard he had held on.

'Saw a mermaid he did, off the Great Banks. That's where they go cod fishing, matey, all among the mists. "Mermaid?" I says when Mike told me. "Too cold for a mermaid there. She'd freeze her tits off, in cold like that".

'But Mike said, "No, she'd got a big fur coat on". Laugh? Ye should've heard me. "That weren't no mermaid," I says. "That were a seal. You forgot what a pair o' tits looks like? How many months you been at sea?".'

Sam is trying to take my mind off the waves, thought Tom gratefully. And it did help to hear a voice in the darkness, one that neither screamed or groaned.

Day after day the ship heaved and dived and groaned, facing seas that towered above it, so powerful it seemed impossible that such a fragile piece of wood could stay afloat. There were days without food now, and even without water, as it was too rough for the guards to venture out on deck.

Tom's tongue swelled in his mouth; his lips cracked. It seemed insane to be so desperate for water when the bilge ran black and foul below them, when water crashed on either side. Days without water – how many days Tom was never sure. How could you know night from day down here, where no light shone and every breath was foul?

The few times sailors ventured to bring them food or water the buckets were plunged down the hatch and everyone was left to forage for their own, instead of having guards to see that it was fairly shared.

Tom didn't have the strength to fight against the adults for food, but he was small enough to wriggle through their legs and scoop handfuls from the buckets into his pannikin and Sam's. He knew his way in the darkness now and it was easier for him to move in the low-ceilinged hold than for the men, who had to crouch double as well as try to stay upright while the ship plunged and shuddered with the waves.

He made Sam drink, too, when there was water to be had. Somehow he knew it was important for Sam to drink. And Sam forced his body to accept the sips of water, the fingers full of porridge or tapioca that Tom fed him.

'Sam?' In the darkness Tom never knew if Sam woke or slept.

'Yes, lad?'

'Are you going to die?'

'Not me, lad. Pickled in saltwater I am. Once yer pickled ye'll never die at sea. Know that fer a fact.'

'Are you sure?' Sometimes Tom felt it would be impossible to face the journey alone, even though it seemed stupid to feel alone crammed with so many.

'I won't leave ye alone, laddie,' Sam wheezed. 'Old marine like me knows all the tricks. I'll see ye through to Botany Bay. Can teach ye things there too. Teach ye to fish, I can. Teach ye knots — now I never did that yet, did I? Find some rag, lad, I'll show ye how ...'

Sam dozed again before Tom could find the rag. Day and night had lost its meaning now. They dozed in restless bouts, then woke and dozed again. But this time Tom woke to find the ship bouncing with the swell, the monster waves forgotten.

'Sam!' He shook the old man's shoulder. 'Sam!' For a second he thought that Sam had died. But then the cracked whisper came again. 'Yes, lad?'

'Is it over?'

'I reckon it is,' said Sam. 'We're in the Indian Ocean proper now. Fair sailing now it'll be, with the wind to our backs.'

Tom nodded. He had learnt to tell wind direction now, by the sound of the sails above them and the motion of the ship. He could tell how much sail they were carrying too, all things that Sam had taught him to pass the time away.

This time, though, Sam was wrong. There were few days now when it was calm enough to allow the convicts up on deck. The winds lashed the waves, even as they sped the ships along.

Now the freezing gales began as they passed into the Southern Ocean, with ice-green water sluicing over the deck and down into the hold, pouring through the deck and hatch so it washed them off their berths and sent foul waves sloshing from one side of the hold to the other, awash with the effluent of humans and sheep.

Once more Tom tied Sam and himself to the berth. 'How soon till we get there?' he demanded.

But Sam couldn't say. They were now in seas far beyond the knowledge of any sailor Sam had known. Only one English captain had sailed these waters before, and he'd been speared to death on another voyage before he got back home.

More and more now Sam muttered in his sleep. Or maybe it isn't sleep, thought Tom. There were times when it was hard to tell if Sam slept or was awake.

'Starvin',' muttered Sam. 'All be starved to death.'

'Give us a break, ol' man!' That from Black Bob, one of the other occupants of their berth. He slid off the berth and made his way across to the almost constant dice game in the corner by the sheep pens, holding on to each berth as he went to keep his balance.

'Sam! Sam, you're dreaming! Wake up!' Tom shook Sam's shoulder. It was probably good for the old man to sleep, thought Tom, but not with dreams as bad as these.

'What?' For a moment Sam sounded as though he knew where he was again. 'What've I bin sayin'?'

'Something about starving,' reported Tom.

'Aye. They all starved, they did,' said Sam vaguely in the darkness.

'Who starved?' demanded Tom.

'The American colony. Every man jack of the first colony, all starved to death. Ship came to take them away, but there wuz none left. Not a single man. All gone to bones they was, in the cold soil. Next colony fared no better. They all starved too, 'cept the Indians helped them ...'

'Sam! Sam! What are you saying?' Tom shook his arms again.

'What? That you, lad? Wasn't saying nothin'. Must've been asleep.'

'You were saying that everyone in the first American colony starved to death,' said Tom fearfully. 'Is that true?'

There was silence next to him. Finally Sam said, 'Aye, matey. 'Tis true enough. But we're not going to starve. All they big rabbits, we kin eat those.'

'They have animals to hunt in America too, don't they?' cried Tom. 'But they still starved to death!'

'Ye'll not starve with Sam next to ye,' said Sam vaguely. 'I'll see ye right, matey. Haven't I sailed the seven seas?' His voice died away again, into a snore.

Tom lay beside him in the rolling dark. He'd been thinking of Botany Bay as a place of plenty, like the ports they'd called in at on the way, with all their vegetables and meat and fruit. But how could there be plenty at Botany Bay? There were no farms, just savages. And he had never known that colonies had starved before.

So far away, he thought. We'll be the furthest colony in all the world. There'll be no-one to help us now.

The ship changed direction. It sailed north now, but the fierce winds still buffeted the fleet and lightning lashed the ships as well, tearing the main yard from one ship and the top sails from another, though the *Scarborough* was unscathed.

And then, again, as suddenly as they had come the winds stopped. The ship rode through a calmer sea and the convicts were allowed up on deck once more.

It took two of them — Tom and John the Tooth, who shared their berth — to haul Sam up through the hatch now. John the Tooth was a thatcher, caught for poaching and transported for fighting the game keeper who caught him. He'd left behind a wife and thirteen children. It was to feed them that he'd gone poaching, as his wages wouldn't feed them all.

Now he would never see them again. Even once he'd served his fourteen years he'd have to find some way to get passage home. Though he'd been sent at the King's pleasure, John the Tooth doubted it would be the King's pleasure to bring him back.

Sam lay in the sunlight in his usual place by the rail. 'We're in the Pacific now,' he muttered. 'Told you that, didn't I, matey? The Pacific Ocean. Nice and quiet it is. I've seen every ocean there is.'

Tom tucked the smelly blanket around Sam and arranged the chains around his skinny ankles more comfortably. Sam shivered in spite of the warm day. 'Good to be in sunlight,' he muttered. 'Don't want to die below.'

'You're not going to die,' said Tom roughly. 'You said you'd see me safely to Botany Bay. You can't go and die on me now.'

Sam's breathing was high and shallow. 'Look at the colour of the water, lad.'

'What about it?' demanded Tom. It looked no different to the waves he'd seen sporadically for seven months. He was pretty sure it was seven — he and John the Tooth had kept count, and they'd known the new year was coming when they'd had a ration of plums and pudding to mark Christmas, and a tot of rum for all the men. He'd given his to Sam.

Sam shut his eyes. 'Means we're near land, that's what it means. An old sailor knows. Look at the birds, too.'

Tom tried to look upwards, though the light still hurt his eyes. What birds? And anyway, Sam's eyes were shut. There was no way that Sam could see birds, even if they'd been in the sky.

'They'll be there, matey,' whispered Sam. 'Land birds — seagulls and who knows what birds ye'll find down here. Bet ye they're up there now.' Sam coughed. 'Give me love to them big rabbits too. You have a roast o' giant rabbit for Sam. Now let me sleep, lad. 'Tis good to sleep in the sunlight for a change. Do me the world of good, the sun.' Sam wriggled to ease his limbs in their chains.

Tom left the old man to sleep. He walked a while to ease the pain in his cramped limbs, and let the fresh salt air soak deep into his chest, then leant on the rail and looked at the thin black line that split the sea from sky.

Where would they first see land? Maybe he would be the first to see it! And suddenly a black spot high in the sky grew nearer, and nearer still, till Tom could see it was a bird, brown and white with wide, stretched wings.

A land bird? he thought excitedly. He turned to Sam.

But Sam's face was covered by the blanket. Two guards knelt beside him.

'Sam!' Tom ran across the deck, as fast as his chains would allow, in between the other convicts who stared at him, then stopped their shambling walk and watched instead — anything that broke the monotony of the day.

'Sam!' cried Tom again. He knelt by the man-shaped bulge under the blanket. The guard pulled him back, gently for once.

'Stand back, lad.'

'No!' said Tom fiercely. 'He's my friend.'

Another guard looked down. 'The lad's looked after him,' he said to the first.

Friends will see you through, Bald Sally had said. Sam had promised he wouldn't leave him, but now . . .

Tom sat back on his heels. Sam had kept his promise: he'd seen him to the new land, or near enough.

Suddenly he felt someone's eyes on him. Tom glanced through the forest of convict legs. The boy Rob stared at him. Was he going to mouth the words 'I'm sorry', as Tom had done to him?

Tom couldn't bear it. That boy had so much, despite his mother's death. He had freedom and a future, his father too, while Tom would forever bear the stain of convict scum.

Tom looked away before the boy could say anything, or make a sign.

'Goodbye, Sam,' he whispered as the guards carried Sam away.

chapter twenty-six

Botany Bay, New Holland
19 January 1788

They sighted land that evening. Again the convicts were confined below, the guard doubled, for once more there was a real chance of mutiny. The convicts now had somewhere to escape to, a land to sail a ship to if they managed to overpower the guard.

Tom lay in the darkness and thought of Sam, and the new land outside he was not yet allowed to see. Even the air that flowed through the hatch smelt different now, carrying an indefinable scent of hot soil and trees.

By mid-morning the next day the ships were anchored at Botany Bay. Five days later they sailed away. All that Tom had seen of the new land were the streams of daylight that flooded through the open hatch, as the convicts waited in the sweltering darkness below.

In the meantime Captain Phillip had found the new land flat and uninviting, too thick with trees and heath to plant their crops.

More importantly, Botany Bay itself was a poor harbour, too shallow to hold the ships in safety, lacking sufficient shelter from the winds that blew from the south each afternoon.

The Indians, too, although they seemed friendly, frightened the newcomers — they were too many, too confident, too naked.

A four-hour sail away, however, was Port Jackson, with its deep inlets protected from the winds, fertile soil, fresh water — and it was invitingly unoccupied. So Phillip made new plans.

Tom was unaware of all this. All he knew was the smell of land, its strangeness even filtering through the stench of filth and sheep; the gentle back-and-forward wash of the ship at anchor; the greater ration of fresh water, and the boredom.

There was no Sam to care for any more. No stories to listen to, no plans to be made. And, somehow, waiting seemed harder now that the end was almost here. Like waiting to go to the privy bucket, thought Tom. You could hold on and hold on, but as soon as the bucket was in sight the pressure was almost unbearable.

It was like that now, but more so.

At last — with no word of explanation to the convicts — the ship set sail just as two French exploration ships sailed into Botany Bay. The English had been just in time to claim the land before the French arrived.

Five hours later they were at anchor again and the guards were detailing men to make the first unloading parties on shore.

chapter twenty-seven

Port Jackson, February 1788

To his intense disappointment, Tom was not assigned to one of the work parties that were the first ashore. He was too young, too skinny, to be regarded as a worthwhile labourer. Nor was Tom present when the colony was formally established in a ceremony on shore on the 26th of January, 1788. Women and children were kept aboard ship until the 6th February, although discipline had been relaxed enough to allow them time on deck.

Tom scrambled up the hatchway and stared out.

The world washed green and blue in front of him, too bright to look at directly after the darkness below. But he could smell the land more clearly now, a scent almost like pine oil but not quite, and the scent of sunlight too.

Slowly his eyes adjusted. He looked around.

His first thought was shock at the wrongness — the too-harsh light, the too-blue depth of sky. And the trees were the wrong colour, a washed-out green; the distance was far too blue, the rocks too golden brown.

The depth of his despair shocked him — had he really expected that somehow this land would be like the country that he had left, his home of two years ago, the village, the hedges, and Pa perhaps, in his printing shop?

It seemed so enormous, the trees — not even the right colour trees — reaching to the horizon. The ships and the settlement on shore looked tiny compared to the vastness of the land.

Courage, he thought. I've survived worse. I'll steal, lie or cheat if I have to, but I'll survive this too . . .'

He felt the warmth of the courage cloak about him, a deeper warmth than the hot sun on his back. And suddenly as he stood and watched, the thought came to him: this land is beautiful.

The harbour stretched out in bright blue fingers, edged with platforms of flat rock and the oddly coloured forest and tiny coves of pure white sand. A flock of birds rose above the trees with weird, harsh cries. They were too far away to see clearly, but Tom had an impression of brightness and unbelievable colour.

Unlike the adults, Tom had not yet been taught what beauty was. Many of the older settlers would never see the slim white trunks of gumtrees, the golden heads of wattle as anything but overly vivid splashes of colour in a barren land. Even the birds were alien, vulgarly bright, their unfamiliar calls too strange to ever think of as musical.

Now, though, when another flock of birds flew by, all green and red and blue, Tom caught his breath. The soft waves slapped at the rocky shores or flopped against sand; the islands sparkled in the harbour. Far in the distance, smoke wafted up softly into the sky.

Something crashed over on the shore. As Tom looked another tree, a monster, came down, its branches smashing as it landed by its brother.

Tents had been erected and already the first few poles dug into the ground for huts. A clear stream twisted between the giant trees, then flowed through mud flats out into the bay. There were camp fires to cook the rations and privy holes and stockyards too, where already the goats and sheep bleated for freedom.

Tom knew how they must feel.

The convicts were only allowed a short time on deck, to smell the air and see the land. With the marines ashore there was more worry than ever that the prisoners might take the ships.

Tom thought that he had grown used to darkness, used to boredom. But it was unbearable now, knowing the land was so close, to sit on the berth — empty now that the two other occupants were ashore — and wait.

Unbearable, pondered Tom. The chimneys had been unbearable. Newgate was unbearable. But he'd borne it.

Eleven endless days passed in the faintly rocking hole below. At least there was always something new to see in the brief hours he was allowed on deck — dolphins playing in the water, an eagle overhead, Indian women in canoes almost level with the water. They seemed to be fishing, though always too far away to see them clearly.

There were smoking fires up on the cliffs at the entrance to the harbour, and sometimes the distant figures of Indians with spears on the far shore. There was the constant stream of long boats ferrying animals, goods and men from ship to land. And all the while the village of tents grew.

On the eleventh day word came for the last of the convicts on the *Scarborough* to disembark — the older and more feeble ones, who had not been chosen for a work party, and Tom. Over on the other ships the women convicts were also lining up on the decks. Tom looked at them curiously. The ships had been too far apart on the vast ocean for him to have really seen the women before.

He'd heard the *Scarborough* sailors say that the women were mostly half-naked on the other ships. But perhaps the *Scarborough* sailors had been jealous of a chance to sail with so many women on board, for these women all seemed fully clothed. Like Tom, they wore hats to shelter from the sun. Even now, in the late afternoon, the sun shone strongly. The air felt hot and moist. Far to the south, clouds massed on the horizon like purple bruises.

Tom waited for the metal collar to be hung about his neck, plus the extra chains he'd worn on land and deck before. Instead a sailor unlocked the chains around his ankles, and shoved him towards the ladder dangling above the ship's boat. 'Move yer carcass,' he said roughly. 'We ain't got all day.'

Boat after boat rowed from the ships. Tom could see the convict women closer now. They were as white-faced as he must be after so many months below. But like him they had done their best for the new land — their hair arranged carefully, tied back with rags or even pinned up onto their heads, dressed in clothes they had kept especially for this day from the store they had been given when the ship departed — as clean as it was possible for them to be in the dark and filthy quarters.

Many of the women carried babies. It hadn't occurred to Tom before that some of the convict women might have children.

Nearer and nearer the sailors rowed. Tom could hear the sounds of land now — shouts and yells and the ring of hammers. There was a strange high-pitched buzzing[6] too that seemed to come from all around. Tom touched the sleeve of one of the sailors and asked 'Please, what's that noise?'

'What noise would that be, lad?'

'The buzzing.'

The sailor shrugged. 'Who knows?'

Tom sat back. The land looked so large, he thought, and the human settlement so small. Finally one of the sailors swung himself over the side of the boat, landing waist deep in the water, and pulled the boat onto the sand. He grinned at Tom. 'You first, lad,' he said. 'Put yer feet on Sydney Cove.'

[6]Cicadas.

Tom looked at the man questioningly. 'That's what the Governor called it,' he explained. 'Sydney Cove, after Lord Bloody Sydney, pox on 'im. It was Lord Bloody Sydney who tried to stop us getting our pay.'

Sydney Cove, thought Tom. A thought struck him. 'Cove' meant 'fellow' in the London cant, as well as bay.

I've lost two friends. I need another badly, he thought. Can a land be a friend?

There was no time for more thought. Tom stood shakily in the rocking boat and made his way to the front so he could jump out without getting his boots wet. There would be no boots to replace them, he assumed, for a long time hence. He landed on the sand, and immediately collapsed almost to his knees. For a moment he couldn't understand what was wrong, but then he realised: for the first time in nearly eight months he was standing on something that didn't go up and down.

He climbed unsteadily to his feet and took one step, and another, the pale yellow sand sinking under his boots. All around him others were stumbling too, trying to cope with the strangeness of solid land, while the sailors grinned as they prepared to row out for another boatful of convicts. Even the cattle in the pens under the trees huddled together as though they dared not take a step.

There were people everywhere — stripping bark from the trees, sawing logs in the new sawpits, stretching dirty canvas over saplings dug upright into the ground to form makeshift tents.

'Listen to me then!' one of the marines yelled. 'Women's quarters that a-way, men over there. Put yer bundles in a tent and wait for orders!'

It was too late to join a work party now. Tom stumbled to the tents and chose the one with the fewest bundles, then lined up by one of the fires for a pannikin of stew, leaning against a tree to eat it.

The stew tasted odd, but not unpleasant. There were strange fresh greens with the barley, and gobbets of fresh meat too, tough and strong-tasting.

Tom wondered if it was from one of Sam's giant rabbits. He'd been looking around for them ever since they'd landed, but with all the human activity there were no strange animals to be seen. He scraped out the last of the stew with his finger, then put the pannikin with his bundle. From now on it would be his, and he'd been warned that if he lost it he'd have nothing to eat from.

Suddenly Tom saw Rob in the distance. He was with two other boys, and for a moment Tom felt jealous again. Rob had friends as well as freedom. Both of the other boys wore the uniform of the marines.

Another of the marines went over to them — the old sergeant Tom had seen with Rob before. The sergeant gave a sketchy salute to one of the boys — even though he was so young the boy wore an officer's insignia and must outrank a sergeant. Then Rob and his father walked up the hill, and were lost to sight among the tents.

Tom gazed around. The shadows had thickened. The wind from the south was cold and strong, and clouds had covered the last rays of the sun. The noise of the camp was louder now. Captain Phillip — or His Excellency the Governor of New South Wales, as he was now — had ordered a ration of hot rum be given to all men and women, convicts too. There was laughter and horseplay, as spirits rose at surviving the voyage and not finding the new land to be the hell that they'd expected.

Tom stayed where he was. He had no wish for either the rum or the revelry of adults. It was already growing dark. It was strange to feel the light change around him, after so long with mostly total darkness and occasional bright sunlight. Slowly it grew softer and softer still, the colours changing as it faded, the yellows turning to greens, the greens to purples. Only the tree trunks still shone white even in the dying light.

An animal screamed in the tree above him. Tom looked up, wondering if there were squirrels in this land too, with louder voices than the ones he knew. But this animal was larger, with wide frightened eyes. It stared at the crowds below its tree and scampered upwards again.

Something rumbled, far away. Thunder. The wind blew even colder. Tom ran back to the makeshift tent and found his jacket and blankets. He put the jacket on and wrapped himself in the blankets, just as lightning streaked across the sky.

Shouts and shrieks ripped through the camp as the

lightning flashed again. Cattle bellowed in terror. Each flash seemed to rip the sky apart.

Then came the rain. It was unlike any rain that Tom had known in England, each drop so sharp and heavy it felt like it could almost rip your skin. It pounded on the canvas roof as men crowded into the small space in the middle that stayed dry.

Then, as suddenly as it came, the rain stopped. Thunder still muttered in the distance; the horizon flashed yellow and blue. But there were stars now as the clouds moved towards the mountains and the wind blew fresh and salty.

Someone threw more wood on the fires. The wood was wet, but the coals were hot enough to dry it. The flames sizzled and leapt orange through the dark. Voices rose around the camp fires again, as the grog was finished.

One by one the men left the tent. There was laughter now, and the sound of shouting from the women's side. Someone was drumming too, and for the first time since the streets of London, Tom heard the plaintive sound of an accordion. Couples stumbled into the darkness, lit by starlight and camp fires. Others danced around the flames.

At least, thought Tom, there would be plenty of room in the tent tonight. It had been two years since he'd had room to stretch out fully and not feel companions' arms and legs landing across him and waking him in the night.

There were bundles of spare clothes and blankets in the tent, where the men had left them before going over to the women's side. Tom wondered what he could steal. He was on his own now. He needed to look out for himself. But when the men came back they'd suspect him of any theft for sure. So he'd need a safe place to store things before he started stealing them. And there'll be time enough for that, thought Tom. This time he would plan things carefully. He'd do whatever he needed to do to survive.

Tom packed his spare clothes next to his body, as Sam had shown him to do to stop others stealing them, then wrapped his blankets around him. It was too wet to sleep at the opening of the tent as he would have liked to do, so he could see the stars.

But at least they are there, thought Tom. I can see them if I want to. Despite the noise from the women's side, despite the strangeness of sleeping on ground that didn't lurch and sway, Tom slept.

chapter twenty-eight

Port Jackson, 20 March 1788

There were six of them in the work party that cut the rushes at the swamps around the harbour, guarded by a young private of marines, with his bright red coat and long-barrelled Brown Bess musket. His job was not to supervise the convicts — Major Ross was very firm that his marines were not in the colony as overseers — but to watch them in case of trouble.

The older convicts in the party were not yet strong enough for the harder work, like digging privies or cutting trees, or the even harder work of sawing the fallen trees into timber, and Tom had been judged too young — so it was the swamps for them. Over a third of the convicts were still too sick to work at all, recovering from the scurvy of the last month of the voyage, or the dysentery which had struck the colony.

The first day the convicts were shackled at the wrists as they hobbled from Sydney Cove to the rush swamps on feet that had known no harder surface than a deck for almost a year and muscles that had wasted as they laid in the darkness of the holds.

But it was two miles to the swamps and the chained convicts made poor time. There were only three hours left in which to cut the rushes and lay them on the rocks to dry out for roofing thatch before it was time to begin the slow walk back in order to make it to Sydney Cove before dark.

The next day the convicts' hands were free. You could almost think we're walking to a picnic by the sea, thought Tom, until he looked at his shrivelled, pale, unshaven companions.

There were better things to look at. The strange trees, lifting their arms to the blue sky. Tom had never known trees to raise their arms before, instead of spreading their branches like skirts above the soil. At night when the moon slanted down through the trees and he peered out through the rips in the canvas tent, he could almost imagine they were about to dance across the rocky ground.

Something thudded through the trees on the slope above them. Private Sharman grasped his musket, then relaxed. 'Kangaroos!' he muttered.

Tom stared. He'd never heard that word before — it was one that Captain Cook had heard the Indians use far to the north. But he knew what the animals were: Sam's giant rabbits, as big as he'd described, bounding away on their hind legs, their long, muscular tails thudding behind them.

Tom giggled — he had never seen anything so ridiculous in his life. Suddenly his spirits rose. It was as though the country had deliberately created silly-looking animals to give him pleasure.

Private Sharman grinned too. He was a young man, no more than sixteen. He carried their rush-cutting knives in a sling on his back, as well as his musket and the bags of shot and powder that dangled from his belt. He had kept a wary eye on the party the day before, especially when the men were issued with their knives.

The other men glanced at the 'roos, then looked away. All of them were Londoners, Tom had discovered, and resented the trees, the animals, the loss of brick and cobbles and the crowded city life they had known even more than their transportation around the world.

The kangaroos — Tom practised the word under his breath — disappeared into the bush. The men straggled onward, down to the bay where the rushes grew thick in the swampy ground.

It was hot work, knee deep in the brackish water. The reeds tore at his hands, still sore from the day before, and his back ached too, and his leg muscles groaned at the unaccustomed labour of walking on land.

But the air smelt of salt and sunlight and the world around him seemed endless. Despite the pain, everything was definitely better than it had been for years — since Pa had died.

Something slithered against his bare leg. Tom looked down, then leapt back.

'Snake!' he yelled.

Private Sharman stood up from his seat on a rock in the shade and ran down to the water's edge to look.

'What is it? Where?'

Tom pointed. 'Snake!' The animal swam between the reeds, then made it to the solid ground and arrowed up the slope. Its back was black and shiny. Its belly glinted red.

Private Sharman squinted at the snake as it tried to hide between two boulders. 'Probably not poisonous,' he said uncertainly.

One of the convicts laughed. It was Black Bob, one of the men from Tom's berth on the *Scarborough*. 'Let it bite ye, matey, and ye'll find out.'

The young marine frowned. 'Back to work, then. No talking or you'll feel the lash.'

The convicts obeyed slowly — the lash was no empty threat. Prisoners had already been chained to the back of a cart and lashed till their blood split onto the new land.

The snake seemed more scared of them than they were of it, so Tom went back to work. Gradually he fell into a rhythm — sweeping with the knife, then catching the rushes before they fell with his other arm; sweep and then with his arms full stagger up the slope and lay the rushes out.

When the rushes were dried they would be carried back to the cove and used for the roof of the storeroom and munitions rooms, still only posts in the ground as wood was cut for their walls.

Suddenly Private Sharman yelled, 'All of you! Up on shore! Knives down on the ground! Now stand together!' He checked to make sure they had obeyed then ran along the beach. He was back a minute later, grinning happily. He held up what he had found: two spears, with strange barbed points, and a stone axe too.

'Must've frightened the Indians off when we approached!' he called, obviously delighted with his find. 'Come on now — back to work! I want the whole patch cut by eventime!'

Tom trudged back into the water. At least it was warm and there were no more snakes. Yesterday Private Sharman had even let them wash before returning. The chimney soot was long gone from his skin. One day, thought Tom, if I scrub enough, the memory of it might vanish too.

Tom glanced back at the marine, sitting on one of the smooth rocks that surrounded the harbour, admiring his haul. He wondered who the Indian was who had lost the spears. Had he been swimming when the men rounded the cove and left the weapons rather than be seen? He hadn't seen any Indians close up yet, though some of the other convicts had, and sailors fishing on the harbour had been pelted with rocks.

Tom hoped the loss of the spears wouldn't stop their owner from hunting, then shrugged — why did he care what happened to an Indian? Perhaps, he thought, he might find tools to steal too. Maybe the tools could even be swapped for money.

The next day was without incident, and the next again. Tom's body was growing used to the hard work now, and to the feel of firm ground under his feet. As they came over the hill to the cove on the third day after finding the spears, Tom saw a canoe resting in the reeds.

It didn't look like much of a canoe in his opinion, just a long length of folded bark, as long as two men maybe and an arm's length wide, tied at the end with dried vines, with sticks jammed along the length keeping the two sides apart. But Private Sharman grinned.

'Look at that!' Private Sharman began to run down towards the cove, leaving the convicts straggling behind him. His spears had been much admired back in camp, as had been the throwing sticks and other Indian goods some of the guards had found or stolen. But no-one had come back to camp with a canoe!

Suddenly, before Tom could properly realise what was happening, Black Bob ran after Private Sharman. He clasped his hands in front of him and raised his arms, then brought them down hard on the marine's neck.

The young man collapsed. His body rolled for a few seconds down the hill, then stopped against a rock.

'What did ye do that for, ye fool?' yelled another of the convicts.

Black Bob grabbed up the sack containing the rush-cutting knives and turned to the other convicts. 'Stop yer complaining! I could've cut his head off, but I didn't.'

He gestured to the bark canoe. 'Who's comin' with me then?'

'Where to?' asked Tom dazedly.

Black Bob laughed. 'China, o' course! China's ten days' sail to the north, didn't ye know?' He looked down at the canoe. 'More'n that in this thing, o' course.'

Black Bob threw the knives into the canoe. 'Well, who's comin'?'

One of the men shook this head. He looked down at the fallen guard, then began to run in the direction of the camp. Two others followed him.

That left one other convict and Tom.

Black Bob looked at the running men. ''Twill take them two hours to tell the news,' he said calmly. 'We'll be long gone by then. Well, you wit' me?'

'I'm with you.' The older convict, Charlie Wilkes, began to stump down to the canoe among the reeds.

'What about you, lad?'

Tom shook his head, confused. Was China really so close? Sam had never said they were near China. In fact, Sam had said they were at the bottom of the world. Botany Bay had sunk, he'd said, when all the other land had floated up. And Sam had seen maps. He'd have known.

And yet ... freedom. Even if they never found China they'd be free. Some of the convicts back at camp had spoken of the two French ships that had met the English ones back in Botany Bay. Maybe the French would take them on as sailors.

'*Gugugu! Wuru wuru!*'

Tom turned. An Indian man ran down the slope towards him.

Tom stared. He'd known the Indians were black, and had seen the women in the distance, but he'd never thought Indians would look like this. He thought they'd be like the Black Man from his nightmares, the one Master Jack had used as a threat for laggardly chimney sweeps, black like the cellar, black as the chimney's soot.

This man wasn't black at all. He was brown, and his skin was shiny as though rubbed with oil. Even more shocking, he wore no clothes at all except for some wooden things hanging from a belt of twisted hair, and the shells and the bones twisted in his beard and hair, and the bone through the bottom of his nose. He was tall too, taller than any man in camp, and more muscular as well, with a cross-hatch of scars across his chest.

'*Wuru wuru!*' he yelled, as though the white men must understand his words. The canoe was either his or he knew who owned it, and he had no wish to see it stolen by Black Bob.

Black Bob laughed. He lifted one of the rush-cutting knives and held it high. The metal glinted in the sunlight. 'Which bit o' ye shall I slice off first?' he taunted. 'An arm, or mebbe your black neck?'

The Indian stopped. Has he ever seen a knife before? wondered Tom. Maybe he has no idea how dangerous such a weapon is.

The Indian laughed. '*Gunin bada!*' he cried. He reached down to his belt and pulled off a length of curved wood, raising it high.

Tom bit his lip. The Indian was going to be killed, and horribly too, with nothing but a stick against a knife! But there was no way that Tom could stop it.

The stick flew through the air. It hit Black Bob on the neck. Black Bob fell, his face and body hitting the water, then lay still.

The Indian laughed again. He grabbed a rock from the ground and suddenly plunged towards the other convict. Within seconds the convict was down, his blood staining the tufted grass.

The Indian turned towards Tom. Do I run? thought Tom, panicking. Will he chase me if I do? There is no way I can run as fast as him!

Tom heard Sally's voice from far away. 'Look small, look innocent. It's yer only chance.'

Would that make a difference to an Indian?

But the Indian had put the rock down. He stared at Tom, as though curious. He stepped forward. '*Guwi?*' He pulled at Tom's shirt till the buttons popped open, then felt his chest and nipples.

Tom remembered someone saying back in camp, 'Poor ignorant heathens, they don't know if we're men or women because we don't have beards.' And Black Bob had grinned and said . . .

'Wha' — what happened?' Private Sharman sat up dazedly and looked around.

The Indian laughed again, though there was nothing funny that Tom could see. He ran down to the cove and shoved the canoe out into clear water, flung himself in and began to paddle.

Private Sharman looked around. 'What …? How …?' He gave a cry and stumbled forward to Black Bob's body, then saw the blood of the other on the ground. He turned to Tom, dazed.

'It was Black Bob,' stammered Tom, wondering if, as the sole survivor, he'd be blamed for the whole thing. 'He hit you, and the others ran off, and the Indian came and —' Private Sharman staggered. Tom ran forward and helped him stay upright.

What do I do now? Tom thought in confusion. Two dead men and an injured guard — what if they blame me?

Even the canoe had gone now. He could still run, but where to, without food or even the means to make fire?

There was no escape. Tom felt Private Sharman lean helplessly on his shoulder. Together they limped back to camp.

chapter twenty-nine

Sydney Cove, 20 March 1788

They took Tom to the new strong room made of rough poles dug into the ground, with more poles from the soft-wooded cabbage trees placed between them to form the walls, which were then roughly chinked with clay. The roof was made of leaves and branches plastered with clay; the door was of rough-sawn planks, but the bolt that stretched across it was strong.

There were no windows. It was the first time since Tom had left the ship that he had been made to sit in darkness. The nights now were studded with stars and he could see the moon slipping slowly through the sky.

Tom shivered as he crouched on his rough stool. Darkness couldn't frighten him now, he told himself. He had survived worse darkness than this. Why should this dark room make him panic now? But he still had to stop himself from pounding on the door and screaming to get out.

If I am ever free, he thought, I will have a house with a hundred candles, and lamps all along the walls. I will never sit in darkness again.

Would he ever be free? Or was Private Sharman now describing how he had been attacked, how Tom had watched and not done anything? Or perhaps he even thought that Tom had killed Black Bob.

One man had already been hung in the new colony. The gibbet had been one of the first structures the English had built in their new land. Tom had watched the execution, like the other convicts, gathered by the guards so they could see what happened to transgressors.

Thomas Barret had been seventeen, six years older than Tom. He had been found stealing butter, salt pork and dried peas. He'd confessed, as Tom had done at his own trial at the Old Bailey, but unlike Tom neither his confession nor his youth had saved him.

Tom had watched the body swing from the gibbet, the dead face swollen and purple, the eyes wide and frightened as though this was just the final terror in the boy's life.

Will that be me, tomorrow? wondered Tom. To come all this way and end like this?

But at least he would die in the daylight and not the night. At least he would see sky and sunlight, and not die in a chimney or the *Scarborough*'s stinking hold.

The bolt that held the door was drawn back. Light flooded in. Tom blinked and tried to see who was at the door.

It was another marine, not much older than Private Sharman. 'Out!' he ordered.

Tom stumbled into the sunlight. Around him the

workers went on, oblivious to his miseries: the convict women hauling buckets of shells from the great mounds the Indians had left on the beach, taking them to be burnt in the lime pits; or others sitting in the dappled shade of the thin, canopied trees, thudding the puddlers in the butter churns.

'Major wants to see ye,' said the marine abruptly. 'Hop to it.'

'Which way?' asked Tom. The tent city was set out roughly in rows and the new buildings fronted onto what would become streets, but it was still difficult to tell where to go.

'That way.' The guard shoved him with his musket.

Major Ross was seated in a square-sided tent, a proper one, not like the makeshift poles and dirty canvas that Tom slept in. His desk and chair were good ones, brought from the ship. Tom had a sudden memory of the magistrate's house, so long ago. The magistrate had furniture like that, too, all dark and shining wood. But the magistrate had looked to be a happier man than Major Ross.

The major was writing something, dipping his quill pen in the bottle of ink, then blotting it neatly before he wrote some more. He glanced up at Tom.

'Is this the lad?'

The marine stood at attention. 'Yessir.'

'I see.' Major Ross put down his pen and looked at Tom. 'Private Sharman has told me what happened this morning. Perhaps you would like to give your version?'

Tom tried to think. What would the marine have said? What story could he make up that would make it all seem better?

Nothing came to mind. Tom raised his chin. It seemed that all he had was the truth.

'There was a canoe, sir, down in the rushes. Private Sharman ran down to look at it. Black Bob struck him down and then the others ran off, all but Charlie Wilkes. Then the Indian came and threw something at Black Bob, and killed Charlie too.'

Tom ran out of breath, the horror chilling him. He had so nearly been killed as well.

'Go on.' There was no pity, and very little interest, in the major's tone. This was just another job that must be done.

'The Indian looked at me. I thought he was going to kill me, too, but then he seemed sort of ... friendlier. Then Private Sharman came to and the Indian took the canoe and I helped Private Sharman back. That's all, sir.'

The major said nothing for a moment. Then he nodded. 'That accords with what Private Sharman had told me. By the way, the other men have not reappeared. I don't suppose you have any knowledge of where they have escaped to?'

'No, sir,' said Tom.

'You were not tempted to escape too?'

Tom considered. Would the major really believe him if he said 'no'?

'Yes, sir. I thought of it,' he said instead.

For the first time Major Ross looked at him with mild interest. 'But you didn't. You stayed and helped Private Sharman.'

'Yes, sir,' said Tom, wondering where this was leading. Not to the gallows, he thought hopefully. No-one seemed to be accusing him of any crime.

'I have heard good reports of you from the *Scarborough*,' said the major unwillingly, as though he distrusted good reports about anything. Who from? wondered Tom.

The major seemed to make up his mind. 'I have received a request that I am minded to agree to. Sergeant Stanley!' he called.

'Sir!' A marine stepped through the door from the far side of the tent. He had evidently been standing there, hidden from Tom's eyes by the wall, listening.

He was much older than the other guards. His hair was grey, his eyes sunk deep in wrinkles and he had three stripes on his shoulder. Tom stared — it was Rob's father!

'Stand easy, Sergeant. Did you hear what the prisoner said?'

'Yessir.'

'And you still wish him to be assigned to you?'

'Yessir. If you please, sir.' Sergeant Stanley looked straight ahead, and not at Tom at all. He was not a tall man, but stood very straight. His eyes were as green as Rob's.

'Very well. It appears the boy can be trusted, to some extent at any rate, if anything in this cesspit can be trusted at all.' For a moment the major's face showed its first sign of real emotion.

The look vanished. The major stared at Tom again. 'You are about to be put into a position of trust. I hope you show yourself worthy of it.' The major sounded more dubious than ever. 'From this time forth you are assigned to the custody of Sergeant Stanley as part of his household. Is that understood?'

'Yes, sir,' said Tom, though he said it only because the major expected it. What did 'assigned to the household' mean?

'Dismissed.' Major Ross looked down at his papers again. Sergeant Stanley saluted, turned on his heel neatly and marched out.

Tom followed him.

chapter thirty

Sydney Cove, March 1788

'Get your belongings,' said the sergeant shortly, 'Thomas — or is it Tom?'

'Tom, sir,' said Tom.

'You're well spoken, at any rate.' The sergeant looked at Tom thoughtfully. 'This were my son's idea,' he added. 'None o' mine.'

'Rob's?' asked Tom, startled.

'Ye've met my son?' The sergeant frowned, his wrinkles falling into new patterns. 'He didn't say so.'

'No, sir. But I know his name.'

The sergeant's expression relaxed slightly. 'I suppose 'tis natural,' he said. 'Two boys of the same age. Well, ye'll be company for him, but I expect you to work too. Are ye a hard worker?'

Tom had never considered it. He'd worked for Master Jack because if he hadn't he'd have been whipped. He'd worked with Pa because he'd loved it. But he knew what the required answer was. 'Yes, sir.'

'We'll see,' said the sergeant, as though he neither believed or disbelieved him. 'Well, be off with you, and get your belongings. I'll see you back here.'

'I'm to go unescorted?' asked Tom uncertainly. 'No guards?'

The sergeant gave a half smile. 'No guards. No chains. If ye plan to run, ye may as well start now.'

'I won't run,' said Tom, and was surprised to realise he meant it.

'Let's hope not, or I'll have egg on me face,' said the sergeant. His voice was hoarse and slightly harsh, as though from years of yelling orders. 'Off with ye now. I've work to do.'

Tom raced past the parade ground and the marine encampment. He guessed that the sergeant and Rob didn't live there. Most families had been given permission to have their own quarters, and even though the sergeant's wife was dead, he still had Rob.

Tom trotted past the women's camp. Already sailors from the ships were digging holes and shoving in posts to build quarters for the women they had grown close to, before they sailed again. He darted into the makeshift tent and grabbed his belongings: the blankets, his wooden bowl and his spoon, the change of clothes, the shoes he rarely wore as already they pinched his feet. Within minutes he was up at the marine encampment.

The sergeant looked him up and down. But all he said was 'Aye, let's go then.'

Tom wondered if they were to cross the Tank Stream, past the gardens that were already being dug by unenthusiastic convicts. But instead they walked around the harbour.

chapter thirty-one

Sydney Cove, March 1788

It was a longer walk than Tom had expected, up the hill and past the work gangs sawing planks and trimming cabbage tree trunks, across a gully of tangled greenery and trickling water, then down again to a small bay with its own tiny beach, no larger than the deck of the *Scarborough*, with wave-smooth platforms of rock on either side.

Tom stared. He had expected a tent among the trees. But here was a house, and almost completed, unlike the settlement of tents and canvas they'd just left.

Sergeant Stanley must have commandeered a squad of convicts, thought Tom, to get a house like this so soon.

Six sets of tree trunks, two in each hole, had been set into the ground, with logs slid between them to make the walls. A door had been cut and propped, and the roof framed too, though it had not yet been covered with rushes. Instead, canvas flapped on the roof beams, tied on with twine.

There was a rough log sheep yard on one side of the house, with two sheep looking hopefully at the new arrivals in case they had brought hay, and a pen with two chickens and a black-tailed rooster.

The sergeant followed Tom's gaze. 'Bought the animals at the Cape,' he said shortly. 'One of yer jobs will be to see them fed. Rob!' he called. 'Where are ye, lad?'

'Round the back!' It was the first time Tom had heard Rob's voice.

The sergeant and Tom walked through the mud to the rear of the house. Tom's mouth dropped open — this was even more impressive than the house.

About half an acre of the gentle slope had been cleared of trees — Tom supposed they had been used to build the house. Three great piles of stumps and roots waited to be burnt. A row of straggly fruit trees had already been planted.

Rob was hoeing the tussocks from newly cleared soil. He looked up as they approached. He looked just as Tom had seen him before, except now he had taken his jacket off, and there was a smear of dirt and sweat on his face as he leant on his hoe. He didn't look particularly welcoming. 'You've got him,' he said flatly.

Like I'm a package, thought Tom, not sure whether to be grateful or resentful.

'I've got him,' agreed Sergeant Stanley. There was a warmth in his gaze that hadn't been there before, Tom thought when he looked at his son. He nodded to Tom. 'Put your belongings in the house, and ye can get to work.'

'Yes, sir.' Tom walked back around the house to the

door and stepped inside. The floor was dirt, as he'd expected, the grass having died in the dim light. A flat, wide stone that would evidently one day be the hearth rested at one end of the house next to a canvas-covered opening in the wall where the chimney would be built.

There were two blocks of tree trunk as stools, and two beds, each made from four rough wooden posts with poles nailed between them, and rope threaded between the poles. Both beds had mattresses of dry grass stuffed into sacking, and rough blankets exactly the same as his.

There was nothing else, except a cooking pot and three large trunks against a wall, propped up to keep the bases from rotting on the damp ground.

Tom left his bundle inside the front door and went round the back again. Rob was back chipping at the tussocks again, and throwing them to one side. This time he didn't even look up.

The sergeant handed Tom another hoe. It looked new.

'Look after it,' he said, and then turned to Rob. 'I'll be back before dusk. Have the fire lit. I'll bring the boy's rations too.'

Rob nodded and glanced at Tom. For a moment Tom thought he might say something — anything — about why he'd asked for him, or even a word of welcome.

But all Rob said was, 'We need to dig out the tussocks. Tree roots too. You start that side. Pile the sods over here — Da wants them to rot down, so he can mix them with wood ash to feed the garden. We need to hurry if we're to get the crops in before winter.'

Tom stared. 'It's not even April yet! It's barely spring.' He wasn't sure why he said it — just to assert himself, perhaps.

'Not here it isn't,' said Rob matter-of-factly. 'It's autumn. Didn't anyone explain it to you? The seasons are upside down here. That's why we have to get the garden in now. Make sure you dig deep — six inches at least. Da says it's no use just scratching the soil.' He bent to his work again.

Tom felt his ears burning with embarrassment. Sam had told him about the back-to-front seasons when they were at the Cape. But he'd forgotten.

He bent to work. Dig, then pull up the sod of grass, shake the soil free and throw it in the pile. Dig again, and shake and throw . . .

He fell into a rhythm, going fast to begin with, to show Rob what he could do, then as his arms ached he worked more slowly, finally finding his own pace. Dig, shake, throw . . .

The garden bed grew wider, and wider still. It will be a good-sized one, thought Tom, remembering the cabbages in the vegetable garden behind Pa's shop, the frost on the leaves and . . .

He thrust the memory away and concentrated on the work at hand. Dig, shake, throw . . . The fresh soil smelt different to the soil at home. It looked dryer, grey rather than black, and crisscrossed with roots even though the main stumps of the trees had been grubbed out.

But at least when he looked up there was the broad stretch of harbour, the ripples dancing, the flash of birds and tumbled rocks like castles along the shores. It was as though his life had suddenly turned to light after the years of darkness.

The shadows were long when they reached the trees that marked the end of the garden. Tom's back ached, the blisters on his hands were even rawer and his stomach yelled with hunger. But he refused to stop. If Rob could keep on going, so could he.

'Water?' Rob thrust a dipper into a bucket of water and fished out a small brown beetle.

'Please.'

Rob took a gulp then handed the rest to Tom. Tom drank gratefully. The water tasted of leaves — the strange tang of this country he was already almost used to.

'Why did you build so far from everyone else?' he asked.

Rob shrugged. 'Da promised Ma a house away from all the lags.'

Lags, thought Tom. That's me.

'There's fresh water here too. Not much, just a trickle down the gully. Takes forever to fill a bucket.' Rob glanced at the setting sun. 'We'd best get the fire going for supper.' He threw a sack over to Tom. 'Clean the dirt off your hoe and put it in the house, then we'll get some wood.'

The freshly grubbed tree roots were still too green to burn, but there was wood in plenty. It seemed that every tree in this land dropped branches, pale cream with grey twigs, and long swathes of bark almost like parchment, it was so pliable and thin. There was driftwood too, strange weathered hunks of wood smelling of salt and seaweed. The boys piled it high near the outdoor fireplace.

'Do you know how to set a fire?'

'Of course,' said Tom, nettled.

'You set it then. I'll get the flint.'

Yes, master, thought Tom. But he didn't say it.

Rob went back inside. Tom shredded bark, then piled on kindling, then bigger wood as well, building the whole into a pyramid shape that would light well. It had always been his job to build the fire at home, and even after two years he still remembered.

But Rob said nothing about the well-set fire when he came outside. He just struck the flint with the back of his pocketknife and watched the spark nibble at the bark, then burst into flame. Rob took the precious flint safe inside as Tom fanned the flame with one of the strange flat sheets of bark. Finally Rob came back, and sat by Tom.

The flames rose and crackled at the wood. Rob threw on more wood. The smoke puffed about the boys, making them cough, then began to rise neatly to one side. The boys sat in silence as the shadows lengthened about the harbour.

'Why did you ask for me?' asked Tom finally.

Rob didn't look at him. 'We're the only boys in the colony,' he said.

'There's a couple of other convict boys. The two marine boys too — the ones I saw you talking to.' Tom flushed when he realised he had admitted watching Rob.

'They're officers. One's the son of the Lieutenant-Governor and one's his nephew.'

'Why can't you join the marines too?' And strut around and wear a fancy uniform, thought Tom, but he didn't say it aloud. 'Because your dad's just a sergeant?'

'I could if I wanted to! But I don't.'

'Why not?' demanded Tom bluntly.

'Because I don't — that's why.' The flames flickered more slowly. Tom threw on more branches. Fires seemed to eat wood more quickly here than back in England. Was Rob lonely, thought Tom suddenly. It had never occured to him that Rob might be lonely too. Was he embarrassed that he'd asked his father for Tom?

'I saw you reading on the boat,' said Tom at last. 'And drawing. Do you want to be a painter?'

Rob said nothing.

'My father was a printer,' said Tom. 'I used to want to be a printer too.'

Rob flashed him a glance. 'What happened?'

'He died. I became a chimney sweep. And a thief,' Tom added.

'We never had our chimney swept at home,' said Rob slowly. 'Da used to shove a goose down the chimney when he was home on leave. Used to flap and flutter on the way down and that'd bring the soot down.

'Poor goose,' said Tom feelingly, remembering the dark chimneys. 'It must have been terrified.'

Rob gave a faint grin. 'Looked stupid though, when it came out the other end. All black and furious. Were *you* terrified?' he added.

'Yes,' said Tom shortly.

Rob looked at him consideringly. Then he stood up, and went into the house without speaking. He was back a moment later with his drawing book. He thrust it at Tom.

'That's what I like to do,' he said, sitting down again.

Tom opened the book. He'd expected to see pictures of the ship, or sea birds, or people's faces.

Instead there were bridges — giant bridges with wide spans, bridges like no-one had built in the world before, thought Tom, or none that he had ever seen. There were buildings, too, some with columns, long windows, strange roof lines. Tom glanced at Rob. He was staring at the fire.

'They're wonderful,' said Tom, truthfully, at last.

Rob's face relaxed. 'You think so?'

Tom nodded. 'Is this what you want to do — build these?'

Rob's face glowed. 'Yes. Somehow. One day ...' He left the sentence unfinished.

They were half a world away from stone bridges and grand buildings, and even Tom knew that sergeants' sons could rarely afford to become engineers or architects. But Tom said, 'You'll do it', and realised that he really meant it. 'You can't dream things like this and not make them real.'

Rob looked at him — really looked at him for the first time. 'I thought you'd laugh,' he confessed.

'Me? No. I'm jealous. I wish I could imagine things like this.'

Rob grinned. 'You stink,' he said suddenly. 'I stink too,' he added. 'Want to bathe?'

'What, in the sea?' said Tom, surprised.[7]

'Why not? It's shallow here, and there's no-one to see.' He got to his feet and ran down the hill without waiting to see if Tom followed him.

Tom caught up at the water's edge. 'It looks safe,' he said cautiously, looking at the dark ripples.

'It's safe.' Rob stripped off his shirt and pants and began to wade in. Suddenly he ducked under the water, then came up spluttering. 'Come on!' he yelled. 'It's warmer in than out!'

Tom stripped off slowly. It wasn't the thought of the water that worried him — it was leaving his clothes. They were all he had, except for what was in his bundle. What if someone stole them while he was in the water?

It was all right for Rob. He had a father to look out for him. If his things were stolen he could get more. The tiny waves lapped at Tom as he waded in, the sand smooth under his feet.

'Come on!' Rob splashed him.

[7]Few English people could swim or bathed in the sea in those days.

169

Tom made to splash him back, then hesitated. This boy was his master, no matter how friendly. Instead he ducked under the water, which was indeed warmer than the breeze, the salt stinging his blisters, and began to wash off the dirt.

chapter thirty-two

Sergeant's Cove, March 1788

The sergeant was unpacking the rations from a sack and placing them in one of the chests when the boys ran up the hill. The chest was raised on blocks of wood set in pannikins of water, Tom noticed, to keep the ants away. Sergeant Stanley must have long experience of making camp under hard conditions

The rations were issued to everyone each week from the stores. The marines and their families got the full ration: two pounds of salt pork each; four pounds of salt beef; two pints of dried peas; three pints of oatmeal; seven pounds of hardtack — the rock-like biscuit that only softened when the weevils had been at it; twelve ounces of hard, strong cheese already turning green; six ounces of butter, and half a pint of vinegar. As a convict Tom would get a third less of everything.

'Da, what's in the other sack?'

'Fish. A big 'un. You eat fish, boy?' he asked Tom in his rasping voice.

'I don't know,' said Tom honestly. 'I've eaten pike,[8] that's all.'

The sergeant shrugged. 'Most o' the marines won't touch it. Fish be good enough if it's fresh and you can soon tell if it's stinking. One of me uncles used to be a fisherman.'

'Da's father worked on a farm,' said Rob. 'Apple trees ...'

'Cider country,' said the sergeant, as though he relished the memory. 'But that was a long time ago ...' He shook his head. 'None of this be getting supper done. How's th' fire?'

Tom looked at Rob guiltily. They'd forgotten the fire. But it was still glowing, with a good bed of coals now. The sergeant nudged the pot, filled with water and dried peas with a slice of salt pork to give them flavour, into the coals then threaded a stick through the fish.

Tom and Rob took turns to hold it above the coals till the skin blackened and the flesh turned white, then pulled the meat from the bones with their fingers as the sun set behind the trees, and the high black sky filled with stars.

'Soon have fresh greens.' The sergeant's hoarse voice broke the silence. He stared up the hill as though he could see turnips growing instead of darkness and the shadows from the flames. 'We'll do some planting tomorrow.'

Tom started — he'd been nearly asleep. The day seemed to have lasted a week.

[8]A freshwater English fish.

'Ye've done well, lads. Time to turn in.' The sergeant pulled a stub of candle from his pocket and lit it on the coals to light their way inside.

Once inside the sergeant glanced at the two rope beds. 'We'll make another tomorrow. You can have mine tonight, boy. I've bunked on th' ground oft enough.'

The gesture touched Tom more than anything in the past two years. But he shook his head, looking at the windowless room and the beds against the wall. 'Sir, may I sleep outside by the fire? I won't escape, I promise.'

The sergeant stared at him. 'If ye choose to escape the door won't stop ye. I don't snore that loud,' he added.

'It's just ...' Tom hesitated. How could he explain that the thought of sleeping in darkness again — spending any time in darkness — made his skin crawl, as though the prison lice were scuttling over him again? He had borne the chimneys, he had borne the dark hold of the ship. But suddenly he felt another night — another hour — trapped in a small space would make him scream.

The sergeant looked hard at him, then suddenly his face softened. 'Dark down there was it, boy?' he said quietly. 'But you ain't sleeping outside. You'll get damp in the dew and get congestion on the lungs or sommat. Nay, we'll keep the door open so ye can see the stars, and tomorrow we'll put your bed by the door. What say you to that?'

'I ... Thank you,' said Tom.

The sergeant nodded, and threw the fish head to the hens.

chapter thirty-three

Sergeant's Cove, Autumn 1788

Tom watched as the sergeant's wrinkled hands carefully dribbled the seeds along the rows in the newly dug garden.

The sergeant had bought his own seeds at the Cape, so he'd have more than the ration given out from the public stores. Many of the officers had brought their own seed to the colony, as well as their own animals — despite the expense of buying hay to feed the animals during the voyage — and fruit trees, and extra shot and powder for their muskets as well.

They were such tiny seeds, thought Tom. Could they really grow into cabbages and carrots, beets and onions, parsnips, melons and turnips? Pa had never bothered with a garden, though most of the other villagers grew their own fruit and vegetables. But here, thought Tom, you grew your own or went without.

The sergeant had already planted the seed potatoes, pressing each tiny seed neatly into the soil, as though this were too important a job to be left to the boys, and the strawberry and rhubarb plants coaxed through the voyage in damp straw.

If the gardens don't grow we'll starve, thought Tom, suddenly remembering old Sam's ramblings on the *Scarborough* about the American colony that starved to death. The garden isn't just serving us fresh cabbages. One day the stores from home will be used up. This land has to feed us now.

It suddenly struck him that in this, at least, he and Rob were the same, or almost: if food ran out the marines and their families might survive a little longer, but in the long run all of them would die.

What if English plants wouldn't grow in this new land? The Indians looked well fed — much stronger than the pale men from London. There were Indians in America too, weren't there? But the white men had starved anyway. Maybe, thought Tom, white men couldn't eat the same food as the Indians.

The sergeant scattered sieved soil on the last of the seeds and straightened up. 'Now, mind what I told ye,' he began.

'Water gently so the seeds don't wash away,' repeated Rob precisely. 'Use the watering can, not the bucket, and make sure they don't dry out.'

'Ye've got it,' said the sergeant. He glanced at the sun rising across the harbour. 'I'd best be off to parade.'

Tom watched him go. There were few parades now — the marines were needed for more urgent work than marching in their bright red uniforms across the muddy parade ground.

There was growing discontent at this. His marines were soldiers, Major Ross said flatly. They were there to defend the colony, not oversee convicts. Despite the Governor's wishes, the marines would only guard the convicts, not check their work or even act as police. If the Governor wanted overseers he'd have to appoint convicts to do the job, not marines.

There was muttering about other things as well: the marines were given the same foodstuffs as the convicts, and Governor Phillip had put restrictions on powder use[9] — even the powder the marines had bought themselves.

There was even more grumbling about the Governor's expectation that the marines would grow their own garden plots — as though they were farm labourers, not soldiers — and that they would eat fresh fish instead of decent beef.

Even if the meat was so hard from months in brine that you needed to sharpen your knife to cut it and your mouth puckered at the taste, beef or salt pork was still the only proper food for an Englishman, accompanied by Johnny cakes baked on a shovel over the coals, or pease pudding, washed down with a mug of bitter grog.

But with his farm and fishing background the sergeant had no such prejudices. He happily swapped the household's salt beef ration for fish, or haunch of

[9]The black powder used to fire the muskets.

kangaroo. You got two giant legs of kangaroo in place of a pound of salt pork, and half a sack of fish instead of a tiny lump of beef which was so old it was almost black, except for the yellow fat and gristle.

The sergeant happily accepted berries and the bags of wild spinach, too, that most of the marines and convicts also refused to touch. The spinach tasted like tin, but it filled you up. There was more food most nights than the three of them could eat, and the hens feasted on the scraps.

'Tom!'

Tom jumped. He'd still been staring at the bare soil of the garden. 'Sorry,' he said. Rob might treat him like a companion, not a servant, but Tom was always aware that if he displeased Rob or the sergeant he could be sent back to the work parties.

He gave the garden one last glance, and followed Rob down to mix more clay and tussock to poke between the logs of the house, to keep out drafts.

* * *

For six mornings after they had planted the seeds Tom woke as the first edge of sunlight inched above the trees, and checked the garden for green shoots rising out of the ground. It still seemed impossible to Tom that seeds carried so far and for so long could grow into food.

On the seventh morning Tom opened his eyes as the laughing birds began to call in the high branches. The sergeant was still snoring across the room, and Rob too, though his snore was more a snort and a snuffle, rather than the full-blown roar of his father.

Tom slid off his bed and slipped out the door before he pulled his breeches on. He rarely wore shoes now. He'd gone barefoot all through the journey so his shoes didn't wear out or rot in the wet floor of the hold before they reached land, but now his feet had grown so much that the shoes were too small to wear.

The first job each morning was to throw twigs on the coals in the fireplace left from last night's log, and pull the big black pot closer to the fire to boil water for tea, or for the sergeant to shave if it was Sunday. But as soon as the fire flickered to life he ran to the garden, peering at the neat, damp rows. They still looked just as they had the day before, bare and brown and ... Tom stopped, and peered closer.

'They're up!' he yelled.

'What's up?' Rob appeared around the corner of the house, yawning as he buttoned his shirt.

'The seeds!'

Rob loped up the slope.

'A whole row of them!' cried Tom, pointing at the tiny spots of green.

Rob nodded, as though he had never doubted the seedlings would emerge. 'Those would be the radishes,' he said thoughtfully. 'And those are lettuces, I think.'

Tom kept staring at the specks on the brown soil. One day, he thought, those will be food.

chapter thirty-four

Sergeant's Cove, May 1788

The colony's vegetables grew, faster and stronger than any plants the settlers had ever seen before. By the end of March the household at the cove had kale leaves to boil with their salt meat, and radishes and turnip tops.

The hens had recovered from the shock of the voyage and started laying. They'd have to save the spring eggs to hatch into chickens, but the sergeant said no hen worth its salt would sit on eggs now. It had been years since Tom had eaten a boiled egg, and that first one tasted better than any he could remember, even though there was no bread and butter to dip in it.

By April the pit toilet had been dug, the roof covered in bundles of rushes, tied tight together to keep the rain out. The boys picked rhubarb for stewing, though it was sour from lack of sugar, and parsley, cress and even a few kidney beans, though the sergeant kept most of the bean crop for seed to plant again in spring.

But the house in the cove still had no chimney. The sergeant had no time to see to it, and he refused to have a convict gang work there without him to supervise.

Now the garden was bearing there was too great a danger of theft.

'Da?'

The sergeant stopped staring out at the harbour and looked round at his son. Sometimes Tom wondered what the sergeant saw as he looked across the water. Not just trees and ripples, Tom was sure. England, perhaps, or the days of his youth ...

'What is it?' asked the sergeant, picking up his spoon and pannikin again. Dinner tonight was boiled 'roo and peas.

Rob glanced at Tom. The two boys had discussed this already.

'Da, can we build the chimney? Me and Tom. I know we can do it,' he added hurriedly. 'I watched how it's done back home and Tom is an expert at chimneys.'

Tom nodded. He knew how to sweep them and repair them, at any rate. 'We can gather the rocks,' he said. 'All we need is some lime.' The colony's lime mortar now came from the lime pits where the convict women brought bags of shells to be burnt and crushed.

'It won't fall down,' urged Rob. 'I promise.'

The sergeant regarded him. 'And if it does it's no great pity,' he said mildly, 'provided and all yer not underneath it at the time. Go ahead then. I'd best be the one to ask for the lime.'

It took a day for the boys to agree on a design.

'Too narrow,' said Tom, looking at the sketch in the sand. 'Be too hard to clean. It needs to be wider here ...'

'But all the heat will fly up it! And it won't draw well.' Rob had studied every detail of every building he'd ever seen. He'd even made a plumb bob from string and bits of lead shot, to keep the chimney straight.

'Then we'll make it taller!' insisted Tom.

'And who's going to lift the rocks all the way up there?' asked Rob.

'We'd need a ladder ...'

Tom but his lip. 'But, we don't have one, do we?'

'We can make a ladder! Look!' Rob made another sketch in the sand.

It took a week to collect the stones, and clean the dirt or lichen off them so the lime could stick them together properly. The few chimneys in the colony were held together with clay and dried grass, except the Governor's, but Rob insisted that theirs would be done properly.

Two days to build the ladder of cabbage tree trunks roped together; three more weeks to build the chimney, wide at the base and tapering upwards, Rob placing the stones neatly while Tom handed them up.

The autumn sunlight glinted off the harbour the day the boys stared up at their handiwork.

'It *looks* all right,' said Rob at last, with his first touch of uncertainty.

'Only one way to test a chimney,' said Tom. To his amazement he felt quite affectionate towards it. He had thought he'd never want to see a chimney again. But in this new land chimneys meant warmth, not darkness and terror.

Tom grabbed leaves and twigs for kindling while Rob gathered larger branches, and they carried the wood into the fireplace. Rob lit the tinder, then they stood back.

The flame struggled, then gusted upwards. One puff of smoke belched out into the room, and then another. The room began to fill with smoke.

It didn't work! Tom glanced at Rob in alarm. Would Rob blame him? Would the sergeant send him back to the labour gangs ...

Suddenly the updraft grew. The fire flared. The smoky room began to clear. Tom let out the breath he hadn't been aware he was holding. 'It's perfect.'

Rob stared at the chimney critically. 'I still say we made it too wide.' He scrutinised the chimney as though still working out how to make it better.

Tom grinned in relief. ''Tisn't. I'll go and get more wood,' he added.

The hens scattered as he made his way past the gardens. It's amazing what hens find to eat, thought Tom. Beetles and grasshoppers and seeds from the tussocks, though they'd had to cover the vegetable seedlings with fishing net to stop the hens scratching them out.

The fishing net had been stolen from the Indians. The sergeant had given the marine who'd stolen it eggs in exchange. There were some thefts, thought Tom as he made his way past the netted area, that the King's representatives allowed.

The garden looked like a real garden now, not a patch of mud among the trees. Each day before starting work on the chimney the boys shovelled the pellets from the sheep yards and scattered them on the soil, bucketed water from the trickle down the gully, mixed the hen manure with still more water into a smelly slurry and trickled that on the garden too.

'Tom? Is the smoke going straight up or to one side?'

'Straight up for ages!' yelled Tom. 'Then the wind blows it away.'

'I *knew* we built it too wide. I bet the rain comes down it! We'll have to make a chimney cap.' Rob's head disappeared around the corner of the house again as he went to rummage for his pencil and paper.

Tom shook the tiny stinging ants off the broken branches then filled his arms with firewood. He stared at the smoke billowing softly from the chimney. I did that, he thought. I made this garden too, and helped put the rushes on the roof. And if we did all this in a few months, what will we have done by Christmas?

He bit his lip. They're not really mine, he reminded himself. They're Rob's and the sergeant's. But despite his thoughts Tom felt his face relax, as though the autumn sun was lending it some brightness.

chapter thirty-five

Sergeant's Cove, Winter 1788

Winter blew in with grey skies and storms that lashed the harbour. There were not enough greens in the public gardens for all the convicts. The convicts, like the marines, had all been assigned space for a garden, as well as given seeds to plant. But few convicts could be bothered, or if they did they only scratched the soil instead of digging deep.

These were men who had chosen a life of theft instead of sweat. Most of the marines, too, felt it below their dignity to grub like labourers in the soil. Governor Phillip ordered search parties to bring in wild vegetables, a seaweed that looked like the samphire of home, and the spinach-like plant that grew along the ground. But many of the settlers, both convict and marine, refused to boil them with their rations. It was proper food they wanted, not the strange plants of an unfamiliar world.

The hospital filled with scurvy patients again, despite the fresh food around them, and the stink of dysentery hung over the new pit toilets.

The wind danced across the harbour as the boys

tramped back to the house from checking the snares. There were fewer fish caught now the cold weather had come, and the hens had stopped laying. Meat from the snares was welcome, but the snares had to be checked at dawn or else the flies laid maggots in the recently dead animals.

Tom wrinkled his nose at the bony little creature in his hand.[10] The last one had tasted like ants. But meat was meat, and there were few larger animals around the settled areas now.

Rob glanced at Tom. 'I thought I'd go and get the rations,' he said. 'You want to come?'

Tom shook his head. Rob needed little excuse to head for the main camp, where he could watch or even help the survey or building teams. But in the camp Tom's clothes marked him as a convict.

The only time Tom accompanied Rob and the sergeant was on Sundays, to hear the Reverend Johnstone's endless sermons about the evils of swearing or the Jesuitical heresy or the dangers of Pelagianism — which few of the listeners had even heard of, and none cared about — and that was only because the sermons were compulsory and no-one except the very sick could escape.

'I'll stay here and skin the critter,' said Tom.

Rob nodded. He wasn't one for talking. Tom watched him stride along the track to the settlement, then went to fetch the skinning knife.

---

[10]Bandicoot or maybe an antechinus.

He didn't even consider staying indoors. Instead he carried the knife and animal up onto the broad rocky platform at the edge of the cove. He was expert at skinning animals now — kangaroos, and wallabies with their dark, too-strong flesh, black swans (the sergeant had shown them how to sew their blankets around the feathers to make winter quilts), opossums.

Tom cut the head and paws off the little beast, then cut around the anus and made a swift shallow slit up its belly, making sure he didn't pierce the flesh. The guts were still warm, and they glistened as they fell out onto the rock. The hens will like those, thought Tom. Now came the difficult bit, pushing his fingers up between the skin and the meat, then scraping off all the bits of fat and sinew, till finally the whole skin lay flat on the rock in front of him.

The pelt was small, but after it dried nailed up on the wall under the eaves he and Rob could stitch it to other skins to make mats or blankets, though the skins would be hard without proper tanning.

Tom sat back on the warm rock and watched the harbour, waving his hand over the meat now and then to keep the flies away. Now there were fewer fish the Indian women spent longer out on the harbour in their canoes with their lines and hooks. Tom began to count: five canoes, six — no, there was another — eight, ten ... each canoe was so low in the water it seemed the women sat on the waves.

How long had the women fished the harbour? he

wondered. Had their ancestors also come as strangers to this place, long ago?

It was strange to think that this country had a history, that it hadn't started when the English ships arrived. Did the Indians have their own stories of times past? But they had no books, or dwelling places, so how could they have history too?

A brace of butterflies, giant blue-and-blacks, fluttered past him. The rock was warm against his skin. Tom was almost asleep.

Craaaawk crawk craw crawrk! Craaaawk crawk craw crawrk!

Tom sat up quickly. Was a native dog after the hens? There'd been one sniffing around a week ago. That was the night the wallaby got into their turnips. Luckily the sergeant could load a musket in ten seconds. He'd got the animal before it had time to bound away, though its meat had been tough and tasted strong and strange.

Tom ran up the beach, then stopped abruptly. That wasn't a native dog! It was a man, bending over among the vegetables in the drab dress of a convict. Two men!

Thieves! thought Tom. They are stealing our vegetabl

Supervision of the convicts was more and more sporadic now. There were not enough free men in the colony to act as overseers, now the marines had refused the job. Governor Phillip had finally appointed convict overseers, and even convict police, but there still weren't enough to keep an eye on everyone, and many convicts refused to obey another convict's orders.

'Stop that!' Tom yelled.

The men straightened and stared down the slope, then grinned, relieved.

'What's it to ye?' yelled one. He was young, though far older than Tom and he was bare chested, his shirt twisted into a rough bag to hold the tiny carrots, parsnips, and potatoes.

'They're ours! Leave them alone!'

'Hush ye mouth, ye little prigger. Ye ain't no better than us.' The man bent down again and pulled up one of the potato plants. The small potatoes dangled from the roots. The man pulled them off and threw the plant away, then bent to pull another.

'Stop it or I'll ...' Tom hesitated. There were two of them and one of him, and they were bigger.

'You'll what? Shut yer gob or we'll scrag and gut you and leave yer doings for the seagulls.'

It was Master Jack's voice, and the voice of the magistrate and the judge who'd sentenced him to exile. It was the voice of all of those who thought that being richer or bigger gave you power — all the power you could get away with using. The other man pulled a carrot, wiped it on his shirt and bit it hungrily.

Courage, thought Tom. I can run and get help, but they'll have gone — with our vegetables — by the time I get back. Or I can do my best ... He glanced down at the bloody knife in his hand. He'd have to get close to be able to use it. He bent and grabbed a branch of wood in his other hand too, then charged.

The branch caught the bare-chested man across the face, leaving a bloody scratch. The man swore, despite the Reverend Johnstone's best lessons, and lunged at Tom. Tom danced back, brandishing the bloody knife in one hand, the branch in the other. 'Get going!' he hissed.

The second man tried to grab him and was rewarded with a poke in the chest. The men stood back now and stared at him. 'Both at once like,' muttered the first man. 'Ye go grab him thatta way . . .'

The men lunged again. One snatched Tom's arm, twisting his wrist till the knife dropped from his hands. Tom screamed. The other man grabbed his ankle and brought him down. He hauled Tom's leg up, as the other grabbed the other ankle, so Tom was upside down, his head dangling just above the soil.

'What should we do with 'im, then? Kick 'is brains out?'

'They'll find 'is body,' said the other, picking up the fallen knife. 'Then it's the gallows.'

'For a brat like this? Ain't like 'e's worth it. If we dropped him off the rocks,' the other mused, 'they'd think he'd drowned, poor mite. Went walkin' on the rocks and lost 'is footing.'

'That'u do it,' the other agreed. Tom felt himself lifted upwards and dragged head first down towards the water, his skull bumping on the uneven path. Think, Tom advised himself. Don't struggle now. Go limp, then when they drop you . . .

'What do you think you're doing?' The men stopped. Tom twisted his head to see. It was Rob, the ration sack in his hand. The first man laughed, but it sounded uncertain. Rob was no convict. Even if he wore no uniform, free men — even free boys — in Sydney Cove wielded authority.

'Run away, laddie!' the man said. But the rough words seemed unsure. 'It ain't no business of yours.'

'They were stealing the vegetables!' yelled Tom, still dangling over the path.

The first man kicked him. 'Quiet! The sprig were misbehaving, that were all. We ...'

'Put him down,' said Rob calmly.

'Look, lad ...' The convict held the knife up warningly.

'You will call me "sir" or I'll have you flogged! Put the knife down.'

The convict hesitated.

'Put it down!' ordered Rob. 'If you try to grab me I'll run, and I can run faster than either of you. And who will they believe — me or you?'

Tom fell in a heap on the ground.

'Now,' said Rob. 'Take off your shoes.'

'Me shoes?' The bare-chested convict stared at the boy. 'But ...'

'I can have you flogged for assault or hanged for stealing food. You saw the hangings last week, I presume? Take off your shoes.'

The men shuffled their shoes off.

Rob spoke clearly and calmly. 'If I ever see you in this cove again you will be flogged, then hanged. Now run.'

The men ran. Rob hurried up to Tom. 'Are you all right?'

Tom nodded. 'Just bruised.' He sat up properly. 'They were stealing the vegetables. But they hadn't got much when I found them.'

'Good.' Rob sat down beside him. 'Are you sure you're all right?'

'Yes.' Tom hesitated. 'I've never heard you speak like that.'

Rob shrugged. 'I never have spoken like that. But I know how it's done. Besides, you're my friend.'

Tom bit his lip. Was he really a friend? If free settlers came in the future, with boys their age, he wondered, would Rob still think of a convict as his friend?

But there was nothing he could think to say, except, 'Why did you make them leave their shoes?'

'They're for you. Yours are too small. It's fair exchange. They were going to steal our food, so we have their shoes.' Rob scrambled to his feet, then put out a hand to haul Tom up. 'Come on,' he said. 'We'd better see what harm's been done before Da comes home.'

* * *

It seemed the only loss was half a carrot. Tom and Rob threw the vegetables the convicts had pulled up into the black pot to stew with the small animal's meat, then rounded the sheep up and put them in their pen for the night.[11]

[11]It would be a long time before fences rather than shepherds kept animals from straying.

Sergeant Stanley sipped from his bowl and nodded. 'Good,' he said.

Tom wrinkled his nose. The meat tasted like beetles this time, he decided, and needed to be chewed for five minutes before you could swallow it. But it was fine to taste carrots and potatoes again, even if they were small. The last fresh carrots he'd eaten had been at the Cape, almost a year ago.

The sergeant wiped his mouth on his sleeve. 'Best keep guard on the place from now on,' he ordered. 'One of you here at all times, the other within earshot, unless I'm here. I'd send a man to help, if I had one spare. But I don't.'

He frowned, his wrinkles deepening. 'The corn[12] crop's failed at Rose Hill,' he added. 'Not one bushel from the lot. Planted too late, to my mind, and not fed nor watered neither. Corn needs muck in this soil. Fools should've known. We'll try some corn ourselves come spring and see if we can do better, if I can get the seed. Might try some maize too.'

He hesitated, for he was a man of even fewer words than his son, then added: 'It makes a difference having you here, lad. I'm glad you've come.' Then, so the hut didn't seem awash with sentiment, he added briskly, 'Don't forget to cover the pot from the flies. We'll have the rest in the morning.'

[12]Wheat was called corn; corn was called maize.

chapter thirty-six

Sergeant's Cove,
December 1788

Spring came with a blaze of yellow blossom. Even the sunlight looked more golden, it was so thick with pollen. The sergeant planted the last of their seed, and the tiny potatoes saved from the early winter harvest. He might trust the boys to build a chimney, but not to plant seeds. If these seeds failed there were no more to plant.

No-one knew what summer might be like in this new country. Winter had been so mild that the greens had kept growing, and the rhubarb too. Would summer be so hot the garden turned to desert? Or so wet that it would rot?

In October the flour ration was cut back, but at the cove they picked spring peas, fat beetroot, giant cabbages and broad beans, and hardly noticed.

The hens turned broody, and fluffed themselves firmly onto their nests of eggs. One week, two weeks, then one hen grew frightened when thunder growled across the cove and let her eggs go cold, so the chicks inside them died.

At the end of the third week Tom gave a yell.

'Rob!'

Rob looked up from his sketchbook. His sketches were smaller these days, as paper was precious. He did most of his drafts now with charcoal on the wide, pale sheets of bark. This sketch was of a Roman bridge, six brick arches over a river, though the only bricks so far produced in this colony were twisted and crumbled.

'The chickens have hatched!' yelled Tom. 'One lot, anyway.'

The boys stared at the balls of yellow fluff peeping out from under their mother's feathery skirts, or staggering out by the woodpile then darting back.

'One, two, three ... I make it fourteen,' said Tom in awe. 'If fourteen hens lay an egg a day,' he calculated, then grinned. 'We'll bust!'

'Half of the chicks will be roosters,' said Rob practically. 'Maybe more. And some may die.'

'Do you think so?'

Rob shrugged. 'Buff Orpingtons are pretty good mothers.'

Tom shot him a look. 'You had hens in England?'

'We lived with Mama's parents while Da was fighting in the Americas,' said Rob shortly. 'They had hens.' He shook his head as though to shake the memory away. 'We can sell eggs to the stores too,' he added. 'And we'll get to eat the roosters.'

* * *

Summer came with thunder that sounded like the harbour's rocks were exploding and rain so heavy each drip stung your skin, and brown trickles seeped through the hut's rush roof. Life had fallen into a routine at the cove now: gathering firewood; fetching water for the garden and the animals; weeding the vegetables; spreading manure on the soil.

Each morning they let the sheep and hens out, to find their own food. The hens come home each evening by themselves, but the boys had to round up the sheep.

It was a lonely life, for Tom. Rob could wander down to the main settlement on the pretext of getting the rations. Sometimes he even attended the regimental dinners with his father.

Friendship? thought Tom bitterly. How could there be true friendship when their positions were so unequal? When, if you angered your friend, he could order you to be flogged, or sent to labour in a work gang? True, Rob never gave a hint of any of this. But Tom was always aware of it. Tom's life was the cove, and his chores. Granted it was a better life than he had known for years, and better than he would have led in a work gang, sharing a canvas tent with the other lags, surviving on the scanty rations or trying to till a garden by himself and keep it from vegetable thieves ...

No, loneliness was better than that, even if the house, the garden and the animals didn't really belong to him. And there was no point dreaming of any different.

* * *

It was December. The maize was high in the garden and the boys were shelling the first of the kidney beans to dry in the sunlight when they heard the thud of someone running up the track. They raced round to the front of the house just as the running man panted to a stop.

It was Private Sharman, whom Tom had helped after Black Bob had attacked him. Private Sharman had called at the hut in the cove several times now, possibly because he felt an interest in Tom's future, but more likely because the sergeant made him welcome and offered him some of their turnip greens and boiled new potatoes.

Private Sharman leant against the hut walls, trying to catch his breath.

'What is it?' cried Rob.

'It's the Indians!' Sharman could hardly get out the words. 'They've attacked the brickworks! Two thousand of them they say, with spears. Your pa's on guard up there!'

Rob looked at him strangely. 'So you came here to tell us instead of going to help?'

'I thought you should be told,' panted Sharman defensively. 'They may attack here as well! It's all His Excellency's fault. Major Ross has warned him time and time again — we need proper military drills! The Indians will murder us in our beds.'

Rob ignored him. His face was pale. He looked at Tom. 'Are you coming?' He began to run along the track without checking to see if Tom followed.

Tom pounded after him, fear clutching at his heart. Private Sharman jogged beside him. Two thousand Indians! How could the colony fight off as many as that? Would they all be murdered?

What would happen to Tom if the sergeant was killed? And what of Rob? Tom thought guiltily. He'd be an orphan too. Tom bit his lip. He was an orphan, and he had survived. At least Rob would still be free ...

They were on the outskirts of the township now, running through the muddy streets that smelt of privies between the canvas tents and identical rectangular huts. Private Sharman veered away towards the marine barracks. Suddenly Rob stopped.

'What's wrong?' cried Tom.

Rob pointed at a figure on the track to the brickworks, his breath coming in loud pants.

Tom peered into the distance, but it was too far away to see who it was. Something about the ramrod walk, though, seemed familiar. 'Your da?' he hazarded.

Rob nodded, his face carefully blank. The more Rob and his father felt, Tom realised, the less they showed on their faces. 'He's all right,' said Rob, still out of breath but his voice almost under control. 'He must have escaped!'

'Yes,' said Tom shortly. Part of him shivered with thankfulness that his life at the cove was safe too. The other whispered resentfully that Rob should have so much, his father as well as freedom ...

The sergeant strode towards them. 'I gather ye heard the news!' he called as soon as he was within yelling distance.

'Private Sharman told us,' said Tom, as Rob seemed unable to say anything. 'He said there were two thousand Indians and they had spears ...'

The sergeant snorted. 'Two thousand! There aren't two thousand Indians in the entire region.'

'But they attacked?' demanded Tom.

'Oh yes. Too many of their nets stolen, too much of their game shot, and I have me suspicions some of the lags have done them even worse. But we shook our shovels at them and they retreated. A lot of fuss over nothing.'

The sergeant suddenly looked even older, as though it hadn't been the Indians' attack that tired him but the quarrels and prejudice of the entire colony. 'Come on,' he said wearily. 'Let's go home.'

chapter thirty-seven

Sergeant's Cove, Christmas 1788

The boys decorated the hut with greenery for Christmas. It shrivelled within a day in the heat, but still looked festive.

Tom woke early, as he always did, and watched the sky turn pink and the sun break through the darker crust of ridge and sea. The boys had made the sergeant's present together: a rack for his pipes and a table to put it on. The table was a bit lopsided, but the rack looked good, and the sergeant looked properly gratified as he hung up his two pipes.

There were clothes for both boys — they'd each grown a head taller in the past six months. Rob said it was being friends that did it — their bodies grew the same — but Tom thought that their bodies simply hadn't wanted to be any larger aboard ship, and had waited till now to grow.

Tom shook his new breeches out. Something thudded on the hard packed-dirt floor. Tom looked at it more closely.

It was a pocketknife like Rob's, a good one.

'Thank you,' said Tom, delighted.

The sergeant shrugged. 'A boy needs a knife,' he said. He reached into the chest again and handed something to Rob. It was long, and wrapped in hessian. 'For you,' the sergeant said lightly, as though the gift was nothing.

Tom watched as Rob unwrapped it slowly. It was a musket. There was a bag of black powder and a larger bag of shot as well.

'Da!' cried Rob, almost speechless.

'Make sure you only fire at what you'll hit,' said the sergeant calmly. 'There'll be no more black powder till the *Sirius* gets back. And if ye don't clean it every time you fire it ye'll feel the back of my hand.'

Rob grinned, and hefted the firearm to feel its balance. 'It'll be the best-kept musket in the colony,' he promised.

The sergeant gave one of his rare smiles. 'Aye, lad, I believe it will be,' was all he said.

Breakfast was Johnny cakes cooked on a shovel over the fire, then over to the main settlement for the Christmas service, as long and boring as ever, the kind-hearted Reverend Johnstone imploring good behaviour from the men and women he would never understand.

For midday dinner there was roast haunch of kangaroo, and boiled pudding made from their own eggs, the weevily flour from the stores and precious sugar and currants that the sergeant had saved just for this day. There were strawberries from the garden, but no-one bothered with potatoes, carrots, turnips or parsnips. Who would want vegetables when you could eat them every day?

The sergeant tipped his tankard of brandy and hot water towards the boys.

'For King and Country,' he proposed, and took a sip.

'To King and Country,' echoed Rob, lifting his mug of water too.

Tom said nothing. Which country? The one he had lost, or this new land? And the King had sent him here, and killed his Pa. But he lifted his mug just the same, and touched it to Rob and the sergeant's. Ideas like that had sent Pa to the stocks. Tom had already lost too much.

Later the sergeant inspected the new leaves of his young fruit trees, then sat with his pipe in the sunshine and stared at the harbour. His face looked calm, but when Tom came out to ask if he'd like another mug he was shocked to see tears on the older man's cheeks.

The sergeant looked up as he approached. 'Memories,' he said. 'There comes a time, lad, when too many of those you loved are gone ...'

I know, thought Tom, images of Pa and Jem before him. But he just said, 'Would you like me to put on more hot water?'

The sergeant shook his head. 'One grog'll do me, lad,' he said. 'Ye go back and keep Rob company. He'll be missing his ma. Dragged her from pillar to post I did, following the flag, never knew what billet she'd have next, hut or humpy or rooms at an inn. Then I had to bring 'em here ...'

The sergeant seemed to remember that Tom was listening. 'Thanks, lad,' he said. 'But there's nothing I want.'

Tom went back inside, where Rob was covering the leftovers to keep them safe from flies and wandering hens.

'He's remembering your mama,' Tom said shortly. No-one had thought to ask him who he missed this Christmas.

'I know,' said Rob. He bit his lip. 'She was his second wife, you know.'

'How did his first one die?' asked Tom without thinking. But Rob didn't seem to mind.

'Don't know. It was years before he met Mama. He doesn't talk of it. Never has. Hunger, maybe. Cold when the army was on the march. I had two older brothers. They died, too, before I was born.' Rob glanced out to where his father was sitting in the sun, his face relaxed for once. 'He always told Mama that one day he'd give her an orange tree. She loved oranges at Christmas time.'

'Do you miss her?' asked Tom, then realised how silly the question sounded. 'I'm sorry,' he said. 'Of course you do.'

Rob nodded. 'She was going to have a baby,' he said. 'That's what killed her. I thought ...' He stopped, then continued. 'I thought Pa might have found a woman here, one of the convicts. Some of the other marines have. But he hasn't. I never knew Pa much till we came here. He was always away. There was just me, and Mama.'

'What was she like, your mother?'

'She laughed a lot,' said Rob. 'And she liked my drawings. She said I'd build the best bridges in the world.' He was silent a moment. 'One day I will,' he added.

'Of course you will,' said Tom fiercely.

Rob shrugged, as though it didn't matter one way or another. Then he said, 'The musket — you can use it too.'

'Really?'

'Of course,' said Rob, as though it had never been in doubt.

chapter thirty-eight

Sydney Cove, March 1789

In the last week of March, when the commissaries came to unlock the storehouse to give out the week's rations, they found half a key stuck in the lock. They reported to the sergeant, who took the broken key at once to Major Ross.

The major looked sombre, the lines of discontent on his face growing even deeper. 'This would indicate, Sergeant, that someone has been systematically stealing food from the stores over a long period of time.'

'Yes, sir.' The sergeant looked straight ahead. Ross was a stickler for discipline, and disliked too much original thought from one who was only a non-commissioned officer.

Major Ross sighed. 'Investigate, Sergeant, and bring the culprit to me.'

'Yes, sir.'

The sergeant did investigate, and found that the culprit was one of his own men. Private Hunt confessed that he had asked a convict forger and locksmith to alter an old key to fit what he said was his sea chest, because he had lost the key. He'd used the new key to steal food from the storehouse.

Seven of them were involved in the thefts, said Private Hunt, one from each of the marine companies. That meant at least one of them would be on guard duty at the storehouse each day, so the others could let themselves in and fill their bags with salt pork, flour, cheese, and the brandy and wine kept for the sick. They had eaten the food, and traded it for clothing and favours from the women.

The men were tried and found guilty. His Excellency Governor Phillip had decreed that theft of food was to be treated as murder, and the sentence for murder was death. The whole colony was ordered to attend to watch them being hanged.

The gibbet had been built at the end of the parade ground. Tom and Rob stood in the crowd, while the sergeant lined up with the other marines as the guilty men were marched to the scaffold.

That could have been me, thought Tom as the first man stepped up onto the platform where the thick noose dangled. They'd have hanged me while half of London looked on.

The Reverend Johnstone spoke a few last words; the prison refused a blindfold. The drum rolled, the rope snapped up.

The marine dangled, still staring at the crowd.

Tom shut his eyes. It could be me. The words jangled in his mind.

He opened his eyes again, but the body on the gibbet still struggled there in the cold wind with the whole colony watching, the marines standing in formation, the loudest of the convicts yelling advice as to how to cheat the devil when they saw him, the women who had been fed with the stolen hoard calling endearments.

Then it was the next marine's turn, and the next. One by one the bodies jerked and wriggled on the end of the rope, before finally, mercifully, hanging still.

Tom glanced around. Some of the convicts were grinning, as though this was the best entertainment the colony had offered yet, as good as the public hangings they'd watched in London. Others shuffled and looked bored, or simply cold, as the noose was slipped around the neck of the fourth man.

It takes so long, thought Tom desperately. Why do they let it take so long?

The fourth body was cut down, and then the fifth.

It was the sixth marine's turn now. His head was down, his face white, refusing to look at the crowd as he was led up onto the gibbet as the last man's body was carried away.

The drum rolled, then abruptly stopped as the body dropped through the trap door. Tom looked away as the man's face began to turn purple, his eyes staring in the sockets, his tongue protruding, his body hopelessly struggling to get free.

There was bright blood on his lips. Tom wondered if the man had bitten through his tongue in his agony, or if a friend had given him a vial of poison to bite into at the end. Poison was a quicker, kinder death than hanging.

Some of the marines in the neat military rows were crying, hiding their faces in their hands. Tom looked away, unable to witness their pain. Of course, thought Tom, they had fought with these men in the Americas, and maybe in the low countries[13] too. Marines were used to seeing their comrades die. But not like this.

Under a giant fig tree His Excellency the Governor watched the executions, his thin face impassive, and next to his lean figure Arabanoo watched as well, his dark eyes thoughtful as he studied the white way of punishment for stealing something as easy to find as food.

Arabanoo was an Indian. Governor Phillip kept Arabanoo a prisoner, and dressed him as a petty officer; he was teaching him English language and English ways, so he would be an ambassador between their peoples.

Well, this is one English way the black man has learnt, thought Tom, as the struggles on the scaffold finally ceased, and the last condemned man was shoved up the stairs to the noose.

* * *

No work was done the rest of that day. The sergeant stayed with his men at the barracks while the boys

[13]Holland, Belgium and Luxembourg.

walked home together. The sergeant's wrinkled face was grave when he walked home in the sunset.

'It's bad, boys,' he said shortly as Tom handed him his pannikin of potatoes and cabbage boiled with shreds of salt pork. The fish had stopped biting lately, and there had been nothing in the snares that morning.

'How much is left in the stores?' asked Rob.

'Not enough,' said the sergeant heavily. 'The governor was right to call those thieves murderers. They've stolen what would keep their friends alive.'

'People are saying we'll starve,' said Rob matter-of-factly.

The sergeant sighed. 'There's food aplenty in this place, but few will eat it. Ye should have heard the men today. They want the rations they are entitled to as soldiers of the King. They want their beef and plum cake, and their grog. Major Ross called the Governor an upstart in front of all the men, demanding what right he had to order that lags be fed the same food as the marines.'

'So we won't starve?' asked Tom.

The sergeant gave a half smile. 'Nay, lad. We won't starve. But we'll need to keep a watch on the garden. Aye, and the hens and sheep as well.'

chapter thirty-nine

Murruroo, Australia,
15 April 1868

Food crammed the sideboard and table, and still new dishes kept coming: dressed crabs and lobsters brought live and clicking in their crates from Sydney giving way to roast goose, stuffed wild duck, and roast chicken with bread sauce, and saddle of mutton with eglantine sauce for those who felt that midday wasn't complete without a slice of sheep.

Roast potatoes, roast pumpkin, buttered parsnips, spinach in cream sauce, cauliflower cheese, the first of the new peas with butter melting into them, then hot plum pudding, apple charlotte dusted with icing sugar and served with cream, strawberry jellies, orange creams ...

It was a long way from the Johnny cakes and pease porridge of the early days, the gruel and weevils on the ship; from Newgate stew or a stale crust of bread.

Thomas Appleby sat at the head of the long table. From here he could see the guests, all thirty of them: family and neighbours (the younger children sat at their own table in the breakfast room), the servants scurrying around with dish after dish, filling the wine glasses, the crystal water glasses.

He could see out the window too, the scythed lawns, the roses brought from England ...

Thomas blinked. Someone was out on the grass, where a second ago there had been no-one at all.

Once again there was an indistinctness about the figure, so it was impossible to almost make it out. Thomas pushed back his chair and stood up to get a better look.

The ghost — if it were a ghost — stared at him through the window. Then Thomas blinked, and it was gone.

He sat down again. People were staring at him. Mrs Henderson touched his hand.

'Mr Appleby? Is something wrong? You look like ...' She hesitated.

Like I've seen a ghost, thought Thomas drily. He gazed down at the table. What would his respectable neighbours say if he told them he had seen a ghost?

Suddenly he thought of Millie, next door in the breakfast room with the other children. She'd go ghost-hunting with him, if he asked. But what if it really were a ghost? It might well be something that no child should see.

Joshua was standing now, raising his glass. 'To Papa!' he announced. 'Many happy returns!'

The others stood as well. 'To Papa!', 'Grandpa!', 'Thomas!', 'To Mr Appleby!', they variously chorused.

Thomas Appleby politely raised his glass in turn. 'To friends and family!' he declared.

No, there could be no ghost-hunting now.

chapter forty

Sergeant's Cove, April 1789

Tom smelt the body as he woke that morning, a strong sweet stench. He sat up and stared out the door.

An Indian boy lay naked on the sand as though he were asleep. But then a ripple washed across the sand, lifted the boy's arm and dropped it, and Tom realised he was dead.

'Sergeant! Rob! Look!' Tom swung his legs off the bed and began to run down to the beach.

'Don't touch it!' Tom halted as the sergeant barked the order. He could see pustules on the body now, thick and crusted red. The salt-laden air was thick with the smell of decay.

The sergeant ran past him onto the sand, and peered at the body himself. 'Back to the hut,' he ordered. 'And don't come close till the tide has swept it away.'

Tom stared. He had seen the scars of those who had survived smallpox in England. He had seen men with syphilitic chancres in Newgate, and the weeping cancerous ulcers of other chimney sweeps.

But he had never seen anyone so encrusted with sores. 'What killed him?' he whispered.

'Could be any of a hundred things,' said the sergeant, in the matter-of-fact tone of one who had seen worse and survived it. 'Poor lad was trying to cool his fever in the waves, I reckon. Captain Tench says they've found dead Indians up the coast too.'

'But we can't just leave him there!' cried Tom.

'Ye can and will,' said the sergeant flatly. 'No-one knows how contagion is spread, lad, but we do know this — them as carries the bodies mostly likely die of the same themselves.'

'Da?' Rob stared out the doorway. 'Are we in danger too?'

The sergeant shrugged. He was not the sort to lie to reassure his son.

There were no more bodies in the cove. But each evening the sergeant brought news of more deaths, whole Indian families dead under the rocky overhangs near the settlement.

'It's smallpox,' said the sergeant heavily, as he shooed a hen off the table. It had been hoping to share their Sunday pudding of salt pork and greens. Most people now boiled their flour with their pork and dried peas, to make it go further, or used it to make Johnny cakes baked on shovels over the fire. But the sergeant liked his meat pudding after Reverend Johnstone's sermon, so they ate potatoes through the week and saved their week's flour rations to mix with the week's salt meat, fresh garden greens, an egg and water, all wrapped in cloth and boiled in the cooking pot.

The sergeant swallowed his mouthful, then cut another slice with his knife. 'Saw Surgeon White after the service. Told me he'd examined an Indian family last week. Whole family with it. Aye, it's smallpox all right.'

Rob frowned. 'Did they catch it from us?'

'They can't have. No-one's had smallpox,' Tom pointed out.

The sergeant nodded. The colony had its hardships, but all agreed it was one of the healthiest settlements on Earth, with no disease apart from the dysentery the first winter. 'The fleet's last smallpox case was at the Cape, seventeen months ago. Nay, Tench says mayhap the French brought it, or Lieutenant Cook's men infected some of the Indians north o' here. Our surgeons brought some scabs, but they are safe in their bottle.'

'Scabs? Why?' demanded Tom, startled.

'Inoculation,' said the sergeant. 'You scratch the skin and run some of the infected matter in, and if luck's with you, you get a mild dose and never get it again. Don't fuss yourselves,' the sergeant said, smiling at their startled looks and reaching for his pipe. 'I'll not be lettin' them try that on you.'

'How do you think it got here, Da?'

'Me? Collins says the Indians have a name for it — *gall-gall*. I bide that it's not the smallpox at all, but a native disease,[14] one that we English don't get. With all

---

[14]We may never know what the disease was, though it seems likely it *was* smallpox. How it came to the colony, however, is still a mystery.

the death about us, not one white at the settlement has gone down with it.'

The sergeant shoved tobacco in his pipe but didn't light it. Tobacco was scarce and the sergeant was hoarding his supply. But he still liked the feel of his pipe in his mouth after supper.

'But I don't want you boys touching the corpses, or even going anywhere near one, ye hear me? If there's one about ye tell me and I'll bring a team to bury it, if the tides don't do the duty first.' He hesitated, then lit his pipe anyway, as though to let the fragrance drive the scent of death away.

Tom shivered. The sea murmured in the background. One of the strange birds yelled in the distance, a hoarse sound more like a scream[15] than a bird call.

What if the disease did spread to the settlement? Would they all die, away from all they'd known? How long would it take for a ship from England to find the dead colony? Or would the new arrivals find only bones gnawed by native dogs, and huts turning back to soil?

[15]Probably a crow.

chapter forty-one

Sydney Cove, Spring 1789

Only one man from the settlement, a sailor, caught the mysterious disease, though the camps of the Indians continued to empty. Even gentle Arabanoo died, finding at last the freedom he had longed for. Although Arabanoo had played with the white children as he sickened, none of the children caught the disease. The plague remained a mystery. Why should the Indians die, and the colonists survive?

In some ways this second winter had been easier for the colony, with greens from the gardens in plenty, and no scurvy or dysentery or any other of the diseases that had beset them after the voyage. As the governor said, the colony was the healthiest place in all the world — if your skin was white.

Indian bodies washed in with every tide now, marked with the red sores of smallpox. The stench of death hung about the colony. The harbour was empty of fishing canoes, as those Indians who could fled inland from the disease, leaving the dying behind them — desperate for water, too weak to find food even if they survived.

The colony's sense of isolation grew amid the death surrounding them. A supply ship from England was overdue. Had their homeland forgotten the handful of lags she'd sent to the other end of the Earth?

Many of the men, and even women, were almost naked now, having traded their clothes for food. The government wheat fields were mostly abandoned. Sydney Cove, it seemed, was not the place to farm wheat.

Only James Ruse, down at Rose Hill (the place the Indians called Parramatta) had luck with his wheat, though he said luck had nothing to do with it at all. It was deep digging and grubbing out the tree roots, scattering wood ash when there was no manure to feed the crops, growing turnips to sweeten the soil.

If you had a garden you were rich — that is, if you knew how to tend it, like the Reverend Johnstone, who had more success with his melons and cucumbers than with his campaign against swearing.

But too many of the marines, and convicts too, refused to dig and sweat to get their food. If the rations weren't enough, they'd steal instead.

Potatoes were treasure now, and like treasure had to be guarded. The boys tended the garden, the sheep and precious hens, and kept watch.

chapter forty-two

Sergeant Cove,
September 1789

The clouds swept above the harbour, leaving islands of shadow and sun. Rob skimmed a stone across the water, and watched it bounce. 'What shall we do?' he asked Tom. It was Sunday, the boys' one free afternoon each week, with the sergeant home to guard the garden.

Tom shrugged. Questions like this irritated him sometimes. He was the convict, and Rob was officially his master. Most times it didn't matter, when it was just the two of them working at the cove. But today they'd been to church service, Rob standing with the other marine families and Tom among the convicts, reminding him again just what he was.

'Don't care,' said Tom.

'Go fishing?'

Tom shrugged again. He'd have rather gone hunting. But there was little powder for the musket now, and besides, it belonged to Rob. Tom used the musket when Rob offered, but he didn't like to ask.

Rob looked at him curiously. But all he said was, 'I'll get the fishing lines.'

Their own cove was too shallow for good fishing, but there was deep water along the coast. You could throw a line off the rocks there, and most times you'd get a nibble in a few minutes, mostly the small, sweet fish with their soft white flesh, but sometimes others too, like the ones with strange flat heads or the ones with knobs like soldiers' helmets. Fish hooks were scarce in the colony now, but the sergeant had shown the boys how to use a thorn for a hook.

Tom recovered his temper as they rounded the headland. It was hard to stay angry with Rob. Rob was like his father: calm and mostly quiet. Tom wondered sometimes if the battles the sergeant had seen — all that violence — had made him quiet in response. Had Rob copied his father's ways? Or was it something born in both of them? Tom thought as they clambered up the boulder that separated their cove from the next. Suddenly he stopped, and held his hand up to stop Rob too.

'Shh!'

'What is it?' began Rob, then he too stared.

An Indian woman was bent over on the rocks beyond them, bashing something with a stone. She was closer to the sergeant's age than their own. A loosely woven red and yellow bag hung from her shoulder. Apart from that she was naked.

Tom tried not to stare at her breasts. Do white women look the same under their clothes? he wondered suddenly. Their skin would be a different colour, of course. But other things ...

Tom suddenly realised there were no girls his age in the colony at all. There were only small children, or older girls, already wooed by men far older than him or Rob. He'd have to wait till the younger girls grew up, he realised, unless more convicts or colonists arrived with girls his age. Strange that he'd never thought of it before ...

The woman looked up. She had a broad scar above her breasts, and there were raised pox scars across her skin. Her skin was shiny from the fish oil most of the Indian women used. Her face looked strange, her eyes puffy. For a moment Tom wondered if she was sick, then he realised she'd been crying.

The woman had seen them, too. She straightened and said something too soft for Tom to hear.

'I think she wants us to go over there,' whispered Rob.

'Why are you whispering?'

'Don' know. Should we go?'

Tom felt a sudden panic, remembering the Indian who had killed Black Bob. But Black Bob had been stealing his canoe and, besides, this woman was unarmed.

She said something again, louder this time. It seemed to be a plea.

Is she alone? Tom wondered. Not just by herself this afternoon — had her family died, her children, her grandchildren maybe? Had they died, while she survived?

'*Ngaawaa!*' The woman beckoned.

Tom slithered down the boulder and began to walk towards her. Rob hesitated, then followed him.

The woman held something out to Tom. It was grey and squishy. Her hand is paler than the rest of her, thought Tom, with two pox scars on the back. The first two joints of her little finger had been chopped off, too, leaving a puckered scar.[16] Tom peered down at the blob in the woman's hand.

'Eeerk,' he said. 'What are we supposed to do with that? Not eat it!'

'It's an oyster,' said Rob slowly. 'I've seen them in London. They're sold in their shells. I wondered if the ones on the rocks here were the same.'

The woman looked from Tom to Rob. Suddenly her tears began to flow again, though she made no other sign that she was crying.

She said something, her voice urgent, and held the oyster up to Tom's lips. She evidently wanted him to eat it.

Would it poison him? Maybe oysters *were* different here. Maybe the Indians could eat food that would poison a white man! Tom looked at the pain in the woman's eyes. He had to eat that stuff, no matter what it did to him. He wrapped the courage cloak around him as the woman held the pulpy mass to his lips.

---

[16]This was done when a woman was promised in marriage.

Tom swallowed.

It was soft and slimy and slightly salty — like a squashed slug, thought Tom. He felt his stomach heave. Was he going to be sick?

His stomach settled again. If the oyster — or whatever it was — was going to poison him, it seemed it wouldn't do it straightaway.

'What's it like?' demanded Rob.

Tom shuddered a little. 'Horrible.'

The woman laughed, even though the tears still streaked her pockmarked cheeks. She bent down again and bashed a shell with her stone, then held the grey meat up to Rob, who glanced at Tom and then swallowed, it. 'It tastes like an oyster, anyway.'

'It was disgusting!'

'Oysters *are* disgusting. But they fill your belly,' said Rob practically. 'People eat them all the time in London.'

The woman held out her stone to Tom. He took it, and as the woman watched he bashed another oyster with it, pulled the shreds of shell out of the ooze, and swallowed, trying not to taste it as it oozed down his throat.

The woman looked delighted. She glanced around her, then beckoned them to follow her.

'Should we?' whispered Rob. Tom hesitated. Somehow it seemed important that they should follow her, though he couldn't explain why. So he just said, 'Yes.'

They clambered across the rocks, then up a gully, with the tall, thick-leafed trees towering above them. The woman reached up and picked something from one of the branches. It was a fruit, hard-looking and brown.

Tom didn't hesitate this time. For some reason the woman wanted to feed them. And he trusted her. She had been so happy when they'd tried the oyster ...

The yellowish fruit was sweet, softer than it looked and filled with tiny seeds.[17] He'd eaten stranger fruits on the voyage out.

Tom nodded at Rob. 'It's not bad,' he said. Rob took one too.

The woman looked as though they had given her a crown of rubies. She laughed again; her teeth were very white. Then she reached up and broke off a giant, brittle branch. Its sap oozed out, thick and bluish white. She began to climb the tree, the weeping branch in her hand.

Up ... up ... She stopped, and rubbed some of the white sap onto one of the branches. Then she let the hunk of wood drop to the ground and clambered down.

She gestured to the boys to be silent.

They sat there, under the giant tree. The wind rustled the leaves above. What are we waiting for? wondered Tom. Maybe more of her family are coming ... But why do we have to be so still?

A wild cheeping filled the air. A mob of the bright birds landed, green and yellow, and began tearing at the fruit.

---

[17]A native fig.

Tom glanced at the woman. They should be keeping the fruit for themselves!

The woman frowned at the boys, as though to tell them to stay still.

Suddenly she stood up. The birds scattered ... all but the ones on the branch where she had spread the sap. Those birds fluttered frantically, but couldn't fly away.

'They're glued to the branch!' cried Tom.

The woman grinned as though she understood his words. She said something too fast for them to make out, then clambered up the tree again. One by one she pulled the birds off the sticky branch, breaking their necks swiftly and flinging them down from the tree. Three, four, five ...

Tom gathered the birds into a pile. Their bright colours looked dimmer somehow here on the ground. Something hit him on the head. He looked up.

It was one of the fruits! The woman took aim and another hit him on the chest, then she began to fling the fruits at Rob too, whatever she could reach. A minute more and she was beside them again. She said something, too fast for Tom to even make out the words. And then she stopped and spoke more slowly, as though the slowness would help them to understand.

'*Dhibilaayn*,' she said. '*Ngina*.' She handed Tom the empty bag.

Tom put one of the birds in it, and when she nodded he thrust the others in too, and the fruit as well.

'I think she wants us to have the bag and all the birds,' he said to Rob.

'That ain't fair,' said Rob. 'It's her bag. And she caught the birds.'

Tom looked at the woman. There was a yearning in her eyes. 'I think she needs to give,' said Tom softly. 'I think ... her children might have died of the sickness. Her grandchildren perhaps. Maybe ... maybe we're the only young people around that she can teach.'

'*Ngaawa*,' said the woman, smiling at them, with just a touch of pleading in her face. '*Ngaawa!*'

So they followed her as the sun rose high above them, then slipped down the sky as the shadows deepened. She showed them how to dig bracken roots to add to the bag with the birds and fruit, and how to suck nectar from the banksia trees; she pointed to the scratches on the tree trunk that meant an opossum slept there. It was so fast asleep it hardly stirred as she wrung its neck.

A large lizard feasted on a long-dead kangaroo. The woman rubbed her stomach.

'I think she means the lizard is good to eat,' said Rob. 'Not the 'roo?'

Rob shook his head. 'No-one would eat that,' he said. 'Except for maggots,' he added.

The woman laughed. '*Buuga-buuga*,' she agreed.

It was a strange afternoon. Looking back, Tom could never quite believe that it happened. Surely they had dreamt it; the woman marching in front of them, her long limbs as strong as the branches of the trees, as she gestured so they would understand. After a while he forgot she was naked, forgot her colour, saw only her strength. This was her land, her knowledge, and for one day she shared it with them.

'*Buugarruu*,' she said, showing them how to shake grass seeds from a tussock.

'*Ganyi*,' she told them, turning one of the big hedgehog-like animals over with her foot.

'The gypsies ate hedgehogs,' said Tom. 'I remember Pa telling me so.'

'Then she means we can eat these too,' said Rob wonderingly, as the woman used a stick to scrape out the nest the spiny animal had been digging in, and crunched some of the wriggling white grubs inside.[18]

There was food everywhere, it seemed. The woman ate as she walked: berries from the narrow-leafed drooping tree that grew on the dry hillsides;[19] gum from another tree, bitter but sweet at the same time; a caterpillar that Tom supposed was no worse than the oyster; then back to the cove next to theirs as she showed them how to dig in the damp sand with a stick to find other shellfish.

There were fruit bats roosting in a grove of fig[20] trees. Fruit bats passed over the cove every evening in a noisy cloud. His Excellency was said to have one as a pet that he fed with rice, but Tom had never thought of eating them. But, '*Wereammy*', the woman said approvingly, rubbing her stomach to tell the boys they were good.

[18]Termite larvae.
[19]Native cherries.
[20]Port Jackson figs, *Ficus rubignosa*.

Eventually the shadows drifted across the ground. Tom shivered. It would be dark soon.

'Rob,' he said urgently.

'What?' Rob seemed lost in a trance of knowledge as the woman moved from one food to the next.

'It's getting late. Your da will be worried.' Angry, too, thought Tom, and he might blame me. 'Do you think ... could we ask her to come home with us? She's so alone.'

Rob hesitated, then seemed to make up his mind. 'I'll try.' He gestured to himself and Tom, then up the hill towards the house.

The woman seemed to understand. But when Rob took her arm, to show her that they wanted her to come with them, she pulled back.

'*Wirraay*,' she said gently. '*Wirraay*.' It was as though she realised that the day had come to an end.

For a moment Tom felt he should kiss her goodbye, as he might have kissed his mother. But he didn't know if Indians kissed and, anyway, the woman was pulling away.

'*Gibirrgang*,' she said softly, already melting back into the darkness.

'Please,' said Tom, even though he knew she couldn't possibly understand him. 'Will we see you tomorrow? Please.'

'*Gibirrgang*,' she said again, and then she was gone.

The boys walked up the hill. A light shone through the door of the house. The sergeant was home already, and had lit the slush lamp[21] for them. Even as the boys looked he peered out anxiously.

'Did that really happen?' asked Rob quietly. Already it seemed so strange as to be unreal.

Tom held up the red and yellow bag. 'It happened,' he said. 'Will your father be angry?'

'Probably,' said Rob, but he seemed unconcerned.

* * *

The sergeant cuffed both boys about the ear, demanded explanations, then cuffed them both again.

Tom didn't mind the cuff, though it made his ear ring. It was the same as Rob received, and besides, he could see the worry in the sergeant's eyes that he would never put into words. Worry for them both, thought Tom. It was good to have someone worried about him again.

The sergeant helped them pluck the bright birds, and gut them too. He seemed to accept the story of the woman without question. But he's seen many lands, thought Tom. The sergeant is more used to strange things than us.

They put the birds to stew in the pot overnight over the banked-up fire, so the maggots didn't get them, and threw the guts out for the hens to eat in the morning. Unlike humans, the hens enjoyed having maggots in their breakfast, and pecked at them with glee.

[21]A wick of twisted wool in a saucer of animal fat: candles and lamp oil were now scarce.

Tom lay on his rough bed and watched the moonlight through the door. It seemed to know its way so certainly up the sky, gliding on like it owned the world. The woman had been like that. So knowledgeable, so secure, as though the whole world was hers.

Which it had been, Tom realised, before the King had sent his soldiers here, and for a moment he felt a sudden hot hatred of the King. This was another evil thing the King was doing — he was taking what was hers.

And yet ... and yet ... Tom wanted to have this land too. A part of it, for him alone. Unlike most of the other convicts and the marines, Tom had no wish to go back to England. There was nothing for him there.

The moon was too high to see now, though the waves in the cove still shone gold in its light. Would they ever see the woman again? wondered Tom. Would she ever see her children either? Or had they been taken from her as her land had been?

Somehow, lying there as the frogs croaked in the night and the bush rats pattered on the roof, Tom knew the answer to both questions.

chapter forty-three

Sergeant's Cove,
Christmas 1789

A week before their second Christmas in the colony, the boys rose in the darkness and jogged inland to a place the Indians had burnt the year before, where the grass grew lush and green. There were usually kangaroos in the early morning there, and by now the boys had learnt to walk softly, with the wind in their faces, so the 'roos could neither hear them nor smell them and run away.

Rob's first shot brought down one of the beasts. Even after a year of practice, though, it still took Rob or Tom a minute to reload, and usually the animals had scattered by then. But this time one of the 'roos doubled back, and Tom felled that one too.

The boys gutted and butchered the 'roos, and scraped the skins clean for tanning, then Rob carried the heavy sack of meat into the settlement to barter it for a piglet from one of the marines whose sow had littered, and who didn't have enough food to feed them all.

The piglet was the sergeant's Christmas present. It was a male, so there would be no pigs bred from it. But once it was fattened they could salt and smoke the neck and back and legs next to the fireplace for ham and bacon. The sergeant loved his bacon. Greens, he said, never tasted right without a scratch of bacon in the pot as well.

There were new clothes this Christmas for both boys, or at least 'new' second-hand shirts and breeches the sergeant had bartered for precious eggs, as there were no truly new clothes left in the colony.

Both boys were almost as tall as the sergeant now. Boys grow tall in New South Wales, said the sergeant wistfully, as though thinking of his other sons, and the child on the *Scarborough* who had not been born at all.

Even for eggs, though, there were no spare shoes or boots to be had. The boys went mostly barefoot now, like most in the colony. Their feet were so tough now that even oyster shells couldn't cut them.

There were no dried currants for the Christmas pudding this year — the sergeant doubted that even His Excellency had currants for his dinner. But the pudding was sweetened with syrup from the beets, and there were two roosters to roast on the spit over the fire, and a giant watermelon.

The year before they had harvested only four melons from their single vine. But the sergeant had saved the seed, and this year there were dozens of melons, and the boys were allowed to eat them as soon as the insides showed a trace of pink.

Later the three of them sat in their rough chairs and picked their teeth and watched the harbour, the too-bright birds sipping at the too-drab flowers, with the sergeant in his stockinged feet chewing the pipe that no longer had tobacco.

'Da!' muttered Rob.

'What is it?' The sergeant sounded half-asleep after the big meal.

'Visitors!'

The sergeant sighed, and slipped his boots on again and laced them.

It was Private Sharman and his wife Mary Anne. The Reverend Johnstone had married them earlier that year, and now Mary Anne held a baby in the crook of her arm. Every woman in the colony seemed to be having babies now, thought Tom without much interest. He stood up politely as the Sharmans approached.

'Merry Christmas to you!' called out the sergeant, then to Rob and Tom, 'Put the pot on for tea, and bring out the leftover pudding.'

Rob nodded without speaking. Tom followed him into the house. Behind him he could hear the adults making small talk, the sergeant politely exclaiming over the baby, and Mary Anne's reply.

Mary Anne had been a convict, a thief like Tom. In England she had been a serving maid in a tavern before being dismissed for being too free with the customers' purses. She was ten years older than Private Sharman. But there were few women in the colony, and Private Sharman was obviously proud that he'd managed to secure one.

Sometimes Tom caught Mary Anne looking covetously at the house and its garden, and wondered if she was planning how to make some of it hers.

'Not while I'm around, missus,' he thought. It had been a long time, he realised, since he'd thought of stealing anything. What was there to steal? Only food and clothes and cooking gear. And he had what he needed of those. There was little actual money to steal in the colony anyway, till a ship brought the marines' two years' pay.

Nevertheless, Tom was still always aware that all he used was only borrowed. It all belonged to Rob and his father, not to him.

'Why do they always come and eat?' he muttered to Rob.

'Because their garden isn't as good as ours,' said Rob mildly, throwing a handful of native tea leaves into the pot.[22] The resulting brew wouldn't taste of much, but at least it looked vaguely tea-like. Rob scooped out three mugs full and carried them outside.

Tom followed with a pannikin of cold sliced pudding. He offered it first to Mary Anne, as the sergeant had instructed him to do the first time Private Sharman had brought his wife to visit. Ladies first, according to the rank of their husbands, then men according to their rank or age, then visitors, then family.

Which leaves me and the hens last, thought Tom, as Mary Anne took the largest piece of pudding. The baby

[22]Indigophera flowers or simlax leaves.

on her knee stared around and burped as she put a crumb of pudding in its mouth.

'It can't go on like this, sir!' said Sharman, continuing the conversation. 'A ship must come soon! We'll starve else.'

Tom snorted, then tried to turn it into a cough when the sergeant frowned at him. What did Sharman know of starving? He was fatter by far than when Tom had first met him, off the ship, and his baby was round and healthy. No, Tom had known starvation, and he didn't see it now.

'We've a ways to go yet before we're in that bad case,' said the sergeant mildly, with another warning glance at Tom.

'But the stores are emptying, sir!'

'Then we'll eat from the gardens, or the forest or the sea. And a few more can grow their own,' he added, with a touch of sharpness.

'But it's not right!' said Sharman earnestly. 'It shouldn't come to this, sir! We need bread, not cabbages and maize cake. We need proper meat. It is our right as soldiers of the King! A man can't live on vegetables and fish!' Sharman spoke as though both foods were unfit for any Englishman.

'They have before,' said the sergeant, his tone even sharper now.

'But, sir,' continued Sharman, then stopped abruptly as his wife nudged him.

'I vow, sir,' she said politely, 'my husband has been telling me such stories of your melons. None have ever seen the like, he says.'

The sergeant sighed and stood up. 'You must take one,' he said courteously.

'Oh no, sir, we couldn't,' began Sharman insincerely.

'I insist. Compliments of the season,' said the sergeant, and led them round the back to the garden.

Later, watching the Sharmans walk back along the path to the settlement, Sharman carrying the melon and a basket of potatoes too, while his wife held a cabbage as well as the baby, Rob said, 'Da — are things that bad?'

The sergeant shrugged. 'People think they are, and that's enough,' he said heavily. 'No, there's no starvation boy, nor will there be, but the feckless are hungry, there's no doubt about that. But what most are hungry for is what they've known — roast beef, wheat bread.'

The sergeant gazed out at the harbour, as though instinctively looking for sails. 'We're hungry for news,' he said softly, and Tom realised that for the first time the sergeant included himself. 'The world could have vanished and we'd know nothing. That's what we're hungry for, lad. And that's something no fishing net or garden can give us.'

chapter forty-four

Sergeant's Cove, March 1790

A malaise haunted the colony now, a depression compounded by fear and isolation.

In February Governor Phillip halved the spirits ration. The sergeant took it philosophically. There was still enough, he said, to enjoy his evening noggin, with a good helping of hot water added. But for others like Private Sharman the loss was yet another sign of how close the stores were to empty, how far they were from the life that they had known.

The Governor took to walking with Bennelong, the new Indian prisoner–translator, up to South Head to stare across the waves, to watch the horizon for the white sails of a ship with stores, but the only sails he saw were those of the *Supply* on her way back from Norfolk Island.

The colony's hunger grew worse, nor was it any easier for being mostly self-imposed. Even the convicts refused to work if they were given maize bread instead of wheat-flour bread, though maize cropped better there than the wheat.

Sometimes, thought Tom, it was as though the settlers were so desperate to impose their familiar standards on this new land that they'd starve rather than accept its bounty.

In March the sergeant came home with news; more than his usual nightly news of the number of bricks made, the children christened — it seemed the Reverend Johnstone had hardly time to grow his cabbages these days, for christenings.

The sergeant sat heavily in his chair. 'The Governor's sending Ross to Norfolk Island.'

'Because the major disagrees with him all the time?' asked Rob. Major Ross still fought the Governor bitterly for more privileges for the marines — for better food than the convicts, a ration of grog for the marines' wives. But the sergeant shook his head.

'Food,' he said shortly. 'There's not enough in the stores to keep feeding so many people. Ross is taking about half the labour force to Norfolk on the *Sirius* and *Supply*, then the *Sirius* is to head to Canton for more supplies.' The sergeant shook his head. 'There's food just for the digging here,' he said. 'There's never been anything like our potatoes in all of England. But the men stand on their dignity, and the officers won't blister their hands but get the convicts to do their work, and half the lags would rather starve than sweat . . .'

Tom flushed. 'Nay, you're a good lad,' said the sergeant absently. 'Now what's for supper, then?'

It was eggs, boiled in their shells in the pot with the chunks of potatoes, turnip, cabbage and carrot. Rob had learnt a little cooking before his mother died, enough to boil a potato or make toast from bread they no longer had in the colony, and Tom had known nothing of cooking at all.

But he remembered. He lay in his bed that night and let his mind roam back. He had hardly ever done that in the old days — it was too painful to wake up to find himself in the cellar, or Newgate, or the heaving hold of the *Scarborough*.

Now, though, with the moon sailing across the sky outside the door, he could remember other times almost without pain. A table spread with a white cloth and a dish of butter, the like of which he might never see again; a jug of cream and raspberries; neck of mutton with an apple sauce; pork trotters in toasted breadcrumbs; apple pudding with hard sauce; toast sodden with butter ...

Would he ever eat those things again? The boiled potatoes they'd had for dinner tonight, the flabby cabbage, the fish grilled over the fire filled their bellies. But if he remembered English food with so much longing — he who had starved for so long that every day it was a joy to feel full — what must the marines be feeling?

And the officers? They must long for the food at home, the days when they were gallant soldiers, not guards of convict gangs digging privies and building walls.

Will there ever be true plenty in this land? Tom wondered. Or will it always be a place where you're sent, convict or marine, to count the days before you can be free and board a ship for home?

chapter forty-five

Sergeant's Cove, April 1790

On April 1st rations in the colony were cut still further to four pounds of flour, two and half pounds of salt pork and one and half pounds of rice per person a week. It was a generous supplement if your garden was producing, if you had fish and the occasional treat of game.

If you didn't have those, however, you'd slowly starve.

Governor Phillip reduced the convict working hours to six a day, so they could work in their vegetable gardens. But for many even looming starvation was not enough to make them work without the threat of the lash.

Worse was to come. On April 5th the *Supply* reappeared — alone — through the Heads. The *Sirius* had struck a reef off Norfolk Island. No-one had been killed, but apart from the tiny *Supply* the colony was cut off from the world, with no hope of outside communication.

Rations were cut yet again, now doled out daily rather than weekly, so the convicts wouldn't eat them all in a day as they had at Newgate. One elderly prisoner died in a food queue with his stomach quite empty. He had lost his cooking utensils, or bartered them for food, and his 'friends' had demanded most of his rations to cook for him.

It was starvation in the midst of plenty. Oysters still covered the harbour rocks; the wild spinach in the gullies grew almost faster than a man could pick it. There were birds to snare and fish to net. It was apathy and depression that was killing the colony now, not lack of food.

Most of the marines went barefoot, threadbare, no more parades or drills. They had become nothing more than convict guards, not the gallant fighting men they had been before, and the thought rankled with them and caused more despair. Were their careers and lives being lost here, among criminals and savages?

They were furious that convicts now had the same meagre rations as themselves, with no distinction for rank at all. Even the Governor took the common rations himself, making over the 300 pounds of flour he had left of his private store to the common store.

Military dinners, the stuff of friendship, were no longer given. How could you give a proper dinner, the marines demanded, with no bread and limited rum, and no great roast as the centre of the table? If they couldn't do it properly, they refused to give dinners at all.

Every garden now had to be continually protected. One man got 300 lashes and six months in chains for stealing twenty ounces of potatoes. There were rewards of food for anyone who informed on food thieves. But no-one raided the sergeant's garden. Even at night now the boys took it in turns to guard it, sitting with the musket across their knees.

It was Tom's turn tonight. He sat on the sergeant's chair under the bark verandah and watched the white foam lapping at the sand. The moon was a cheese rind on the horizon, enough to turn the ripples silver. Behind him the sergeant's snore filled the hut, with Rob's snore underneath it, a quieter version of his father's.

Tom felt his eyelids close. It did no harm to doze on these night watches. If anyone tried to steal the hens the clucking would rouse him soon enough, or the sound of digging from thieves at the potatoes. A few minutes' sleep was all he'd take …

It was half an hour perhaps before he opened his eyes again and stared.

The moon had made a golden highway across the water. It seemed to lead to their cove alone, as though calling him to cross the water and sail up through the sky.

But there were figures in the waves. At first he thought they were people splashing in the shallows, potato thieves perhaps. But why would potato thieves frolic in the water?

Then he realised what they were. It was a mob of kangaroos, four of them — no, five — a giant male, three females and a younger 'roo, who splashed as delightedly as all the others, its coat a flash of brown and silver in the moonlight.

It was impossible. It was ridiculous. It was the most beautiful and amazing thing he'd ever seen.

For a moment he was tempted to call Rob and the sergeant, so they could see the splashing animals too. But no matter how softly he moved he might frighten the 'roos, and besides, if the sergeant wasn't caught up in the magic of their game he might see nothing but roast kangaroo, grab the musket and fire on all that beauty ...

Tom must have made a noise, for suddenly the big 'roo cocked his head and gave a short sharp bark. The mob scattered, the females to either end of the small cove, the buck hesitating before he followed them.

Suddenly the cove was empty.

Should I have shot one of them? thought Tom dazedly. It had been weeks since they'd had a big piece of meat to roast. They could have salted some as well.

No, he realised. There was no way he could have pulled the trigger. For tonight, watching the mob of 'roos, he had known the animals had everything he wanted — a family, laughter, freedom to bound through the bush and keep on going, with no-one to answer to but themselves. Freedom to bound over the mountains even, to find the world beyond.

Tom settled back in the chair, the musket still on his lap. One day he would shoot kangaroos again. He'd eat their meat. But he knew he could never look at them without remembering their beauty, without thinking, yes, that is how I want to live.

chapter forty-six

Sergeant's Cove, May 1790

The colony's gloom grew. The malaise swept from person to person, growing deeper week by week, caused not by lack of food itself, but lack of food from home, of the security of food in storage, of news from England, of any feeling they were not abandoned by the world, to starve or to survive. Did the world even exist beyond Sydney Heads?

The French Revolution had swept that country's king from his throne; England was at war with France; the United States of America had its first president. But the young colony knew none of it.

It was a town of mud and rags. There was no starvation. The hospital still had no cases of pellagra from lack of protein, scurvy, or other diseases of hunger. But many believed that they would starve.

Rain blew in from the south and stayed, bringing grey skies and grey harbour, winds that lashed the huts and stripped the bark from the roofs and the mud from between the wattle branches in the walls. The streets were deserted.

Down at the cove the hens stopped laying in the wet, and fat drops oozed through the roof, even though the sergeant had replaced the old rushes with new shingles. The hut now had a stone-flagged floor, and even a verandah roofed with bark where the sergeant could sit with his pipe after supper. The garden flourished despite the unrelenting wet; the sheep and hens were multiplying; they even had the first apples from the tree, and the sergeant had taken his largest potato last Sunday to compare it with Reverend Johnstone's and, to his delight, had found that his was bigger.

But even at the cove the greyness took its toll on the sergeant and the boys. Now they too watched the harbour, waiting for the sails that never came.

chapter forty-seven

Sergeant's Cove, Winter 1790

'Tom!' The word was hissed.

Tom looked up from the patch of cauliflowers he was weeding. The rain had stopped, at least temporarily, and they were taking advantage of the dry. The cauliflowers were hearting nicely, he decided. 'What is it?'

'Sshh!' Rob pointed over towards the trees. His hands were muddy, the fingernails black with dirt these days.

Something stared at them. Something taller than the sergeant, with beady eyes and thin grey legs, and a body covered in brown feathers that looked entirely too big for those legs.

'Emu,' whispered Rob. 'Da said the bad weather has forced them back this way. I'm going to try to creep inside and get the musket.'

'If you move you'll scare it!' hissed Tom. But Rob was already moving stealthily, head down, through the vegetables and round the corner to the front door.

Tom glanced back at the bird. It cocked its head as it regarded Rob's departure, then looked back at Tom. It seemed quite unafraid.

It stepped forward, stopped, then stepped closer once again. It bent its head and pecked at the lettuces, chomping almost half a lettuce with every bite.

Tom's first instinct was to yell at it. But they needed meat more than lettuces. The meat on that giant bird would feed them for a month.

Where was Rob? Surely he'd had time to load the musket with shot and powder now!

All at once the emu looked up. *Blam!* The musket's yell echoed around the cove. A mob of cockatoos rose screaming from the trees and the rooster crowed in alarm.

It'll frighten the sheep too, thought Tom automatically as he watched the emu fall. We'll have to round them up before they go too far.

The scent of sulphur lingered in the air. The fallen emu twitched. Its long legs pumped the air, as though trying to run. But it was too late to run anywhere.

Tom got to his feet. 'Nice shot!'

Rob grinned, but didn't say anything. He stepped up to the emu and prodded it with his foot. Despite the twitches it was clearly dead.

'Blimey,' said Tom suddenly. 'It's going to take us hours to get those feathers off!'

It took an hour to pluck the bird so they could gut and butcher it. Clouds had blown up in the late morning, with gusty drizzles of rain, so they sat by the doorway. The wind was strong today, but hopefully the worst of the emu fluff would blow out, not in.

Meanwhile, the pot bubbled on the fire, filled and refilled with seawater. Once the water was boiled down to a froth so salty an egg could float on it, they could soak the surplus meat in it. The salted meat would keep for a month, or more if the weather stayed cold. The boys had never eaten emu before, but the sergeant had, down at the mess, and said that it was good, without the rank flavour of a lot of this land's meat.

Feathers flew everywhere. Long, brown wing feathers, almost too tough to pull out, fat body feathers, fluffy pin feathers — at least a million of them, thought Tom. There were enough feathers to stuff an entire quilt, if only they had material to put round them. But they could stuff more into the quilts already on their beds, or maybe the sergeant would barter them.

'Tom! Tom, look!'

'What?' Tom gazed down the cove, expecting another emu.

But Rob was staring out through the Heads.

Tom followed his gaze. At first he thought he was imagining it. They had dreamt of ships arriving for so long; had imagined every cloud on the horizon must be sails.

But this was real. A ship, its tall sails like cockatoos flying against a blue sky.

'A store ship from England,' breathed Rob, staring at it like he expected the sails to fade away to clouds.

'I'll stay here,' offered Tom, 'if you want to run over to Sydney Cove.' He still hated being in the main settlement. When I'm free, he thought, I won't mind being seen. Lately he had started to count the months till his freedom. He had served nearly four years already. Only forty-four months to go.

Rob glanced at him, then shook his head. He bent again to the plucking.

Tom sighed. Sometimes he wished Rob would use just a few more words. 'Look, I'll be fine here. You don't want to miss the excitement.'

'That's all it'll be,' said Rob calmly. 'Just excitement, no real news. No-one will really know anything till the Governor's told. I'll go down tomorrow with Da. He'll know what news there is tonight.'

Tom gazed out at the ship again. It had changed tack, and was making for one of the coves just inside the Heads. A few seconds later it had vanished.

Had it really been there? Or had he imagined it? But Rob had seen it too.

Tom glanced at Rob, intent on his plucking, and grinned. Rob would never imagine a ship. He was too practical. The only things Rob imagined were his buildings. Lately he had been making models from twigs and leaves stuck together with brittle wattle gum. Tom knew how badly Rob missed sketch paper and his pencils.

The emu was finally plucked, then gutted, leaving a huge mass of stinking entrails. The hens pecked at the guts warily till the rooster tried them, then they were all at it, swallowing the bloody gobbets and spreading the mess across the soil.

Rob used the hatchet to cut up the bird, while Tom threw small pieces into the saltwater — if the chunks were too big they'd rot before the salt could penetrate — then threaded the giant legs onto the spit and set the fire under it. The meat hissed and spat as the oils and juices dripped into the fire.

Tom sniffed. 'Stinks a bit.'

'So do we,' said Rob, smelling his hands. 'There was some sort of oil in those feathers. Or the skin maybe.'

'Wash?'

Rob nodded.

It was too cold to swim. The boys stripped off their shirts and scrubbed themselves with the wet sand, then splashed themselves clean. The world smelt of wind and salt and the whiff of cooking meat from up at the hut. And hope, thought Tom gazing out at where the sails had fluttered. There's a smell of hope as well.

* * *

The sergeant came home earlier than usual. Tom expected him to look elated at the arrival of the ship, but his face and tread were heavy.

'Da! What's wrong?' Rob asked.

The sergeant glanced at the lumps of roasted meat on the spit above the coals, the potatoes baked in the coals and dusted free of ash and, warming on the hearthstone, the boiled greens in the pot.

'Rob shot an emu,' said Tom, as proud as if he'd shot it himself. 'There's three buckets of meat salting too.'

The sergeant nodded. 'Good,' he said distractedly.

'Da? The ship?'

'The *Lady Juliana*. It's pulled up nearer the Heads — the wind's too strong for it to come to harbour. Tench and some others took a boat out and went aboard. It ain't good news. More than 200 women convicts. More useless mouths, that's all.'

Tom gaped. 'No stores?'

'Some. Not much. There were another ship, the *Guardian*. She struck an iceberg. They abandoned her at Cape Town. She had two years' supply of stores on board.'

Tom glanced at the buckets of salting meat, the good food by the fire. 'Sergeant — we have enough. We'll survive.'

'Oh aye,' said the sergeant heavily. 'There's food enough for them as has the wit to stretch out their hand. But can the Governor keep order? Folks want what they've always known, not emu and wild spinach. They want salt beef and flour. They want clothes and powder for the muskets and shoes and candles too.' He shook his head. 'I simply do not know. They say there are more ships coming. P'raps they'll bring relief.'

'Paper,' said Rob. 'We need more paper too.' Every inch of his sketchpad was covered now, back and front and margins. He sighed and turned the spit to brown the emu legs on the other side. 'A ship of women. What use are they?'

The sergeant looked at him sharply for a moment, but said nothing.

chapter forty-eight

Sergeant's Cove, 12 June 1790

She came along the dusty path from Sydney Cove, carrying her bundle of clothes and blankets, and staring about her. In spite of her ragged clothes and too-white face she was pretty, thought Tom, her black hair combed up and held neatly with a piece of rag. He stared at her over the bucket of turnips he'd been cutting for the sheep.

Had he looked like that two years ago? he wondered, pale and sunken-eyed from the ship's hold, still walking unsteadily after so long at sea, and gazing like he expected the trees to bite him or the Indians to charge across the hill?

'That must be her,' said Rob calmly beside him. Tom glanced at him. It was impossible to tell what Rob felt, nor had his face shown any emotion when the sergeant told them over breakfast that he had requested that a convict woman be assigned to him.

'Ahoy!' Tom yelled.

'Ahoy yerself.' The woman stepped down towards them. 'This'd be Sergeant Stanley's place then?' She looked at it appraisingly. 'And ye'd be Rob and Tom?'

'I'm Rob,' said Rob impassively. 'And this is Tom.'

'I'm Emma Mason. Pleased t' meet ye, Tom.' Her voice was pleasant too. Tom wondered what she'd been transported for. She smiled, as though she knew what he was wondering. 'A poisoner,' she confided. 'Poisoned seven husbands and me landlord afore they got me.'

She grinned at the boys' faces. 'Green as cabbages, ain't ye? I was a pickpocket, and a good one. Could slip the readies from yer pocket afore ye even knew that I was there. And ye?'

Tom flushed. After his first confession he had never referred to his crimes in front of Rob. 'Theft,' he muttered.

'Well, I didn't think ye were a rapist or a murderer, laddie,' said the woman good-naturedly, making Tom's flush even hotter. 'I'll just put me things down, shall I then, and ye can show me around.'

'You show her,' said Rob shortly. 'I'll feed the sheep and fetch t' water.' He grabbed Tom's bucket of chopped turnips and marched over to the sheep yard. There wasn't enough grass about the hut now to feed the sheep in mid-winter, so the sergeant had suggested feeding them turnips and barley hay, as well as chopped leaves from the berry trees[23] in the gullies. Rob dumped the bucket full of turnips, then tramped off through the trees.

Tom turned to Emma. She looked at him, amused. 'Seems His Highness don't like a newcomer,' she said casually.

[23]Probably lillypillies or kurrajongs.

Tom shrugged. He led the way up to the hut. It looked very different now from the rough structure of two years ago, with its shingled roof and wattle branch chairs out the front. The garden out the back was fenced now to keep out the sheep and hens, its rows of muddy cabbages and carrots, strawberries, beetroot, sugarbeet and radishes, rhubarb, spinach, turnips, endive and winter lettuce neat in the sun. Though most of the fruit trees were leafless, they were taller than Tom now and held the promise of summer apples, figs, pomegranates, oranges, pears, quinces and plums.

It was dark inside after the winter brightness of the cove. Emma gazed around, taking in the table and chairs, the chests, the three beds, the flat hearthstone and the cooking pot suspended over the glowing coals in the fireplace, the hooks the sergeant had carved and nailed on the walls for their clothes. 'Very nice,' she said. She sounded surprised.

'And this is the storeroom.' Tom opened the door with pride. They had only finished the new room in the autumn. It was almost as big as the hut itself. Emma stared at the sacks of potatoes, the huge turnips, baskets of maize cobs and dried beans and peas, the pumpkins hanging in nets from the ceiling, the buckets of salted emu meat.

'*Very* nice,' she said again, but this time she sounded both impressed and relieved. 'Ye do yerself well here.'

'Well enough,' said Tom shortly, watching as Emma surveyed the main hut again. Finally she put her bundle on the table.

'Are you hungry?' asked Tom reluctantly. Rations had been reduced in the settlement again, and he guessed that Emma wouldn't yet have friends who might offer her food from their gardens.

'Famished,' said Emma frankly.

There wasn't much to offer her. Even in winter the flies laid maggots in any cold meat left for more than a few minutes, so they cooked it as they needed it. But there were cold potatoes left from breakfast, and Tom toasted a hunk of emu over the fire.

Emma munched the potatoes and gazed at the meat hungrily as it cooked. 'The master won't give you the lash for this, will he?' she asked warily. 'I wouldn't want ye hurt, lad, for feeding me without permission.'

Tom looked stonily at the roasting meat. He had never even thought to ask permission for anything he ate or offered others at the cove. He had grown used to the privileges of almost-freedom, he realised. It made him uncomfortable to hear Emma remind him of his true position.

'I won't get into trouble,' he said flatly, and handed her the meat.

It was almost too hot to touch but Emma gulped it down, as though worried that someone might appear to take it from her before she could finish. Then she wiped her mouth on her ragged sleeve.

'Well, I'd better be lookin' useful when His Lordship gets back, or he'll be tellin' his father on me,' she said. 'What can I be doing?'

'The sergeant usually brings the rations home with him each evening,' he said noncommittally.

'What sort of a master is he?'

Tom swallowed. Nowadays he was able to forget for hours at a time that the sergeant and Rob were his masters. 'Good enough.'

'No beatings?'

'No beatings,' said Tom. 'He expects us to work hard, though,' he added.

'That's no worrit to me,' said Emma calmly. 'And I told him so to his face. This is a new country and a new chance and I'll not be missing it. So, what do ye usually have for dinner then?'

'There's emu,' offered Tom. 'It's best roasted, I think.' He saw the look in her eyes.

'What the holy blazes is emu then?' Emma demanded.

'You just ate some. It's a bird. The meat's all right, as long as you roast it so the grease drips out. It tastes funny otherwise. I can show you how to cook it if you like.'

Emma burst into laughter, genuine and friendly. 'I'll call ye my brother if ye do, lad! For I ain't cooked a thing in me life.'

'But ...' Tom hesitated. All the women in his village had known how to cook. But Master Jack's fat Lettice, he remembered, had lived on the hot potatoes, the thin

255

stews and chestnuts and bread of the streets. There had been no stove to cook on at Master Jack's, and Emma was London bred too.

They were by the cooking fire when Rob came in, with Tom showing Emma how to turn the meat on the spit. Tom glanced at Rob. He'd been away much longer than it took to fetch more water. Rob looked over at Emma's bundle on the table, then back at Tom.

'We'd better gather up the sheep,' he said.

Tom nodded. There were nine sheep now, and more lambs to come this spring, and they were wandering further and further afield to find patches of grass.

'I don't suppose you can spin?' Tom asked Emma.

Emma shook her head, her eyes laughing. 'That I can't. Where would I get a sheep in Spitalfields?'

'Come on,' said Rob impatiently, not looking at Emma. They stepped outside, then stopped. The sergeant was coming home early. And he was leading a cow with a young calf at its heels.

'Da!' Rob seemed to forget Emma's presence for a moment. 'How did you get that?'

'For two bags of potatoes and another of corn and our pork ration for two weeks. It was cheap enough. The owner didn't have grass enough for it any more. It should eat the same leaves as the sheep, with luck, and we've turnips enough to feed it.'

The sergeant stared at Emma, watching silently from the doorway. 'Well, Mason, can you milk a cow?'

'No, sir,' said Emma. She seemed more timid

suddenly, now the sergeant was home. She patted her hair carefully to make sure it was still in place.

'Make cheese? Butter?'

Emma shook her head.

'I'll have to show you then,' said the sergeant calmly. He glanced at the sun, still a hand-span above the far-off mountains to the west. 'Look lively, boys and go and strip some wattle branches. If we bend our backs to it we can have a pen for the calf built before supper.'

'What about the cow?' demanded Rob.

'She won't stray far from her calf. Let her roam as long as she doesn't take to coming inside. Don't neither of you feed her near the door so she doesn't get ideas.' The sergeant handed the cow's rope to Rob. 'Tie her up, will you, son? I'll just dump these inside.' He held up the bag of rations, then ducked his head under the lintel and stepped inside. Tom watched his gaze fall on Emma's bundle on the table.

'I weren't sure where to put me things, sir,' said Emma, gazing at the sergeant out of the corners of her eyes. She sounded half-shy, half-defiant, thought Tom.

The sergeant didn't look at her. 'In the storeroom,' he said. 'Ye can have my mattress in there for tonight. We'll make you your own bed tomorrow. Be sure you keep the door shut though, to keep the rats out.'

Emma looked at him speculatively. Then she said, 'Yes, sir', and went to gather her belongings.

The sergeant glanced around, and saw Rob staring in the doorway, the cow behind him. 'What are ye waiting for?' demanded the sergeant.

Rob gave his first smile since Emma had arrived. 'Nothing,' he said, and went to tie up the cow.

* * *

A mopoke hooted beyond the hut. Tom could hear the ripple of the waves. The ripples sounded louder at night. It was funny, he thought, how you noticed sounds more at night.

Something rustled across the room. Tom strained his eyes in the darkness. The sergeant softly got out of bed, and walked out the door beyond Tom's bed.

Tom glanced over at the dark shape that was Robe's bed. Was the sergeant going to Emma? Had Rob noticed? Tom listened for the soft cluck that Rob made when he was asleep. But there was only silence.

Was that the storeroom door opening? Or just the sheep moving in their pen? What if . . .

A shadow darkened the door again. The sergeant stepped quietly across the floor and got into bed. Within seconds he was snoring.

He only went out for a wee on the fruit trees, thought Tom in relief. Across the room, from Rob's bed, came the sound of a soft sigh. Then the hut was silent, except for the patter of the bush rats in the shingles.

chapter forty-nine

Sergeant's Cove, June 1790

Breakfast was subdued, no-one said much as they ate their cold potatoes and roast emu, and drank their mugs of native tea. Emma made a face as she sipped the tea but said nothing, looking sideways at the sergeant as Rob turned the slab of emu on the spit.

Later, after the sergeant had shown them all the rudiments of milking a cow and left for work, and with Rob out checking if the hens had decided to lay a winter egg, Emma turned to Tom as they chopped the leaves and turnips for the animals. 'The sergeant, is 'e normal then?'

Tom blinked. 'What do you mean?'

'Fancies women, that's what I mean. He ain't had his cods blown off, or like that?'

'No,' said Tom shortly. 'His wife died on the voyage out.'

'I knew a cove had his cods blown off,' said Emma reminiscently. 'He'd been in the Americas war. An' I've known coves miss their missus too much to marry again, and all. What do you think, lad? Is there any chance for me?'

Tom pretended not to understand. 'Chance of what?'

'Don't play the fool. With the master.'

'I think,' said Tom carefully, 'that he'd have gone to you last night if he was going to at all.'

'That's what I thought,' said Emma thoughtfully. 'Damn. An' I thought I was onto something, gettin' meself assigned to him. Best be lookin' elsewhere, then.' She looked at Tom frankly. 'There ain't many women here just now. Most of the ones I sailed with are off to Norfolk Island. Now's the time, I reckon, to find meself the best cove I can.'

Emma glanced at her reflection in the bucket of water by the table, and smoothed her hair. 'Do you think the young master'd mind if I took a walk down to the settlement this afternoon? Fetched the rations, like?'

'I think he'd agree,' said Tom slowly.

Emma grinned at him. Her teeth were good, with only a few gaps at the side. 'I'll let ye know what I find.'

chapter fifty

Sergeant's Cove, June 1790

It took Emma exactly a week to find herself a husband: one of the gardeners who worked for His Excellency and had his own hut behind Government House, plus meat from His Excellency's shooter and all the vegetables he — or Emma — wanted.

It only took another week for her to have him in front of the chaplain, with the sergeant and Tom and Rob in attendance, and a wedding feast of roast black swan (a gift from His Excellency), a cake made of maize flour, and potatoes, parsnips and broccoli from the Government House gardens.

'Ah, it were a grand wedding,' said Emma happily the next day. 'And Bill is a grand man. Why, he's twice the man me first was.'

'Your first what?' asked Tom cautiously.

'Me first husband, o'course.'

Tom stared. 'Is he dead?' he demanded.

'Not that I know of, bad luck to him,' said Emma calmly. She grinned, and winked at him. 'But who's to know he's not, so far away 'n' all? Now off with you. If ye've nothing better to do you can build me a new hen house.' Emma had taken to the hens, and was indignant on their behalf at their crowded conditions.

'Rob and I were going to shear the sheep,' said Tom dubiously. The last time it had taken both of them to hold one sheep down while they clipped off its wool in ragged chunks. 'Anyway, the hens like being crowded together at night.'

'Asked 'em, have ye?' retorted Emma, picking up the empty bucket to take down to the cove to gather oysters and pippies. Oysters were the one thing Emma knew how to cook, throwing them into the pot with milk and chopped potatoes. It seemed her sister was a fishmonger, carting her barrow of oysters through the London streets. Oysters were grand food for a husband too, Emma added, with a wink neither of the boys understood.

Tom watched her trudge down to the sandy shore. Was Emma's marriage legal? Probably not, he thought. But maybe few marriages in New South Wales were. And Emma was happy, and so was Rob, and the sergeant ...

Tom hesitated. *Was* the sergeant content? With a flash of insight Tom realised that after a life spent marching from battle to battle, with two wives who had spent their lives either trudging behind the army or longing for their husband, perhaps the sergeant had decided that one more close relationship was more than he wanted to handle.

Tom opened the chest and took out the shears, greased with rooster fat and wrapped in flannel to stop them rusting. He was content, too, he realised suddenly. He was happier than he had ever been in his life before.

chapter fifty-one

Sergeant's Cove, 30 June 1790

The end came unexpectedly, out of the black night. Tom was almost asleep when he heard Sergeant Stanley's firm footsteps along the track. He had warned the boys that he would be late tonight: he had a meeting with Captain Tench and then a dinner with the other marines.

Usually when he came home late he doused the lamp he carried, and found his way to bed by starlight so as not to wake the boys. But tonight he hung the lamp from the rafter and stirred up the fire so it sparked and spat.

'Da?' Rob blinked and sat up in bed.

'Ye'd best get up,' said the sergeant heavily. 'You too, Tom. This concerns you as well.'

Tom slid out of bed and slipped on his jacket. The breeze from the beach was cool and so were the flagstones under his feet. Rob wrapped his blanket around his shoulders and sat on the edge of the bed in his nightshirt. 'What is it, Da?'

'You didn't see the ships come in?' Another ship, the *Justinian*, had sailed into harbour a week before, bringing welcome stores and the news that three more ships of the Second Fleet were approaching. It had seemed to the inhabitants of Sydney town that their shortage might soon be over.

Tom shook his head, disappointed. 'We were hunting. We got a kangaroo,' he added. He didn't say that he had been the one to fire the musket. 'We promised Emma she could have the skin for a mat.'

'Good,' said the sergeant absently.

'Da, what's the news?' demanded Rob.

'The *Neptune*, *Scarborough*' — Tom flinched at the name of his old ship — 'and *Surprise* are in,' said the sergeant shortly.

He shook his head as the boys looked eager. 'No, not good news. The worst it could be, almost. A thousand convicts they sent us, but a quarter died on the way. Starved, poor creatures, their teeth rotting in their heads from scurvy. All the sick and helpless in the Thames' hulks, that's what they thought to give to New South Wales this time. Ain't a single able-bodied man among them.'

The sergeant shook his head at the memory. ''Twas as bad a sight as I 'ave ever seen, and I were twelve years old when I joined up. We had to lift the lags from the decks to get them to the longboats, all blind in the bright light and moaning fit to break yer heart, spitting out their teeth and ulcers weeping from what flesh they 'ad. Couldn't hardly stagger, most of 'em. They'll be months recovering, if indeed they ever do. I'm glad that ye weren't there to see it.'

Tom sat wide-eyed. How would the colony cope with hundreds of sick and helpless? But Rob was staring at his father. 'Da, what else?' he pressed.

'The fleet brought two companies of soldiers too,' said the sergeant briefly. 'The New South Wales Corps, they're called, formed especially for the colony.'

Rob looked at him sharply. 'Good men?' he asked, with all the authority of a marine's son.

The sergeant laughed shortly. 'Good? They're men who'd be accepted in no other company in the world. Scum of England, beggars and blackguards every one, and the officers no better. They signed up to do any job that's wanted of 'em: gaol warden, juror, foreman of the privy diggers — they'll do it all.'

'Will you be in command of them?' asked Tom.

The sergeant poured more water into the cooking pot and shoved it onto the hob before he spoke. 'That I'm not. We marines are being shipped back to England, as soon as the ships sail again,' said the sergeant briefly.

'No!' The cry stunned Tom with its terror even as he uttered it.

'Tom —' began the sergeant.

'No!' cried Tom again. He wanted to yell, *No, you can't leave me alone! Pa, Jem, Sam — they all left me! You can't desert me too!*

But there was no point saying the words. Of course Rob and his father could leave him, just as Private Sharman would leave his wife, just as the whole marine corps would leave their temporary lives in New South Wales behind.

Rob and the sergeant owed him nothing. Rob had given him friendship, the sergeant food and shelter, and Tom had given his own friendship and work in exchange. But they were not his family. And he was a convict and bound to stay in the colony for another three years.

Instead he ran. Ran out the door and down the moonlit path to the cove, stubbing his toe and wrenching his knee as he tripped on rocks, on tree roots. Finally he stood by the black rippling waves, feeling the soft sand between his toes, the humped rocks on either side looking more like sleeping camels than ever in the golden light.

Should he run further? Why stop now? He could make his way by moonlight down the coast. He'd be well away by morning, and neither Rob nor the sergeant would believe that he'd escaped till long after he'd gone, well into tomorrow.

He could get away from them all, away from Sydney Cove. Join the Indians, perhaps. Maybe they would be kind to him, welcome him, as the Indian woman had so many months ago.

Maybe . . .

Tom shook his head. Courage, he thought. I need the courage cloak more than ever now. Because I can't run. I have only three more years and a bit to go. No matter how bad they are, I can survive them.

And then I will be free.

Tom shut his eyes and felt the cloak's soft warmth around him. Three years, he thought. And maybe they won't sail for another few months. And the sergeant will speak well of me. Perhaps I can be assigned to help with the vegetables on Garden Island, or go down to the Rose Hill Farm.

It would mean leaving the house he'd worked to finish, his own bed, the garden they'd watched grow. Never seeing Rob or the sergeant again, as they sailed to another life, leaving him behind.

I have survived worse, he thought. I can take this too. And then I will build myself another life. A good one.

Tom opened his eyes. And slowly it seemed that the gentle night had become part of his cloak, the moonlight and the soft hush of the waves, the scent of leaves and salt, the heart of New South Wales.

I'll still have this, thought Tom. Sydney Cove, my friend Sydney, my friend New South Wales. This land, at least, will never desert me. This is what I'll build my life on, he thought. The land.

Tom turned to walk up to the house again. Rob touched his arm. Tom hadn't noticed him standing quietly behind. 'Come back to the house,' he said softly.

'I was going to.' They walked in silence.

The sergeant had put the pot on the fire to brew sarsaparilla tea for the boys and a hot rum for himself. The mugs were warming against the flames. He turned as Tom and Rob came in.

I'm not going back with them,' he told Tom bluntly. 'I'm resigning from the marines.'

'Resigning?' stammered Tom. 'But . . .'

'This will be a good country.' The sergeant spoke vehemently, as though to convince himself. 'There's going to be a bad year or three, I can see that. But there'll be free folk coming out in a few years and there's land aplenty for us.'

He gave a wry smile. 'What's there for us back in England? War with the French again for me, and after, if the Frenchies don't shoot me arms off or leave me with one leg, a poor old age starving on half pay. And there's no money to get Rob taught his engineering.

'Nay, I've spoken to the Governor. He and us marines 'ave 'ad our differences, but he's done his best, and it ain't been easy.

'The place to go is Rose Hill. The soil's good there, by the river, and there's easy water for the fields too. I'm to get a land grant, just down from Ruse's farm. They say his wheat's a sight to be seen, and his maize crop too. He's a good man when he's not on the drink. We'll have a farm to begin with, grow apple trees, maybe build an inn one day. They'll give me a team of convicts too, and rations for them, to get established. Free labour. That's how America got rich, with slaves.'

So that was what the sergeant dreamt of as he looked across the waves, thought Tom. Apple trees.

The sergeant caught Tom's eye. 'Aye, lad, I can see what yer thinking, that ye've been a slave yourself. But soon enough ye'll be free and ye'll get a team to work yer land in turn. That's the difference between slave and convict, see? Nay, it'll be hard work. But I have a feeling we'll do well.'

'We ...?' Tom met his eyes.

'The three of us,' said the sergeant clearly. 'You're family now, son, if ye want to come along.'

Tom could have sung for joy, or flung himself into the sergeant's arms. But it would have embarrassed the sergeant — and he had no song to sing.

So he just said yes, and grinned.

They drank the sarsaparilla tea that still tasted of nothing in particular, and the sergeant sipped his weak rum and water slowly to make it last. The moon sank behind the house; an owl began hooting its strange night song.

'You know,' said Tom into the silence, 'I think I'd like to raise sheep one day. Lots of sheep.' It was the first time since Jem died he had dared speak of the future.

'Sheep!' Rob considered, and shook his head. 'Sheep smell, and they're brainless. They'll need bridges down at Rose Hill. And proper buildings one day. And I'll be there.'

Tom grinned. It seemed foolish to dream of fine bridges and grand buildings in a settlement of huts and rags. But they had already come across the world, and they'd survived. Nothing was impossible tonight.

'Dreams,' said the sergeant. But he sounded hopeful, rather than dismissive. 'Dreamers, the lot of us.' He smiled at the boys. It was the widest smile Tom had ever seen him give, as though at last life was opening its doors for the sergeant too.

'Come on,' he said. 'It's time we got some sleep. There's work enough tomorrow.'

And the day after, and the days after that too, thought Tom. The years stretched in front of him, filled with sunlight.

Murruroo, Australia, 1868

The land had been generous to them all, thought Thomas, as he sat on his verandah and listened to the neighbours leaving in their carriages and sulkies, the clatter of the teacups, the laughter of the children as they ran along the river.

Four years more had made the colony a place of abundance, not privation. Rob had built his stone bridges, and his grand buildings too. Rob's buildings would still be standing, thought Thomas, long after Rob's name had been forgotten. But Rob wouldn't mind that. The best of him, he'd said, was in his buildings. It had been fourteen years since Rob had died, at the age of seventy-six. Thomas still missed him.

The sergeant's inn had flourished. People called him the sergeant all his life, for he'd looked like a sergeant still, and spoke and moved like one too. The sergeant had taken Emma with them, with her Bill assigned as one of his convict team; and although Bill had turned to rum when he was given emancipation, and their own land grant eventually had to be sold, as James Ruse's had been, he'd proved a competent enough foreman when he was sober.

And as for Tom ... When he was freed in 1797, Tom was granted land down river from the sergeant's and assigned convicts to work it, too. In 1815 he sold his farm, and was one of the first settlers across the Blue Mountains. By 1825 Thomas Appleby, who had once been an almost-slave, had 4000 acres, a team of forty convicts, and neighbours who had never heard of a convict boy called Tom ... and he had Eliza.

Thomas smiled in memory of Eliza. Like him, she'd come to this country by herself — but free, not as a convict. She had courage, his Eliza. Millie had a look of her, something about the hair and chin. Eliza knew he'd been a convict. And she'd smiled and said, 'You're what you ever were. You're a good man, Tom.'

Thomas Appleby shook his head. He'd loved Eliza, but she'd been wrong. London, Newgate and the chimneys had stripped the goodness from him. It was this country that had given it back, this generous land that had given him so much.

So many countries, so many faces, all within his early years. Then fifty-five years in one place, learning its winds and its seasons. Drought and flood, then gold, the greatest flood of all, men from all over the world marching down the road to make their fortune or creeping back, despairing.

They'd sold mutton to the miners, and pit props too. And then there was the Crimea and men needing uniforms — all the wool in the world it seemed had been needed for the army. Gold had made the Applebys comfortable; the war had made them rich.

'Mr Appleby!'

Thomas opened his eyes and sighed. 'What is it, Miss Hildegard?'

'It is Millicent! I really must protest.'

'What has she done now, Miss Hildegard?'

'She was riding a sheep, Mr Appleby!' said Miss Hildegard virtuously, and waited for the old man's look of horror.

Thomas tried not to grin. 'Tell her to come to me,' he ordered.

Millie wore her buttoned boots. Her blue silk dress was crumpled. Thomas tried to look stern. 'Millie! What's this about you riding a sheep?'

'The boys dared me,' said Millie simply.

'Do you always do what they dare you to do?'

Millie considered her answer. 'Sometimes.'

Thomas came to a decision. 'Millie, have you ever been scared?'

'No,' she replied firmly.

'Not about anything?' pressed Thomas gently.

Millie hesitated. 'You won't tell?' she said finally.

'Cross my heart,' said Thomas.

'You've got to spit three times to make it true,' instructed Millie.

Thomas spat on the verandah floor.

'I'm scared of the bunyip pool,' admitted Millie. 'I'm scared ...' She hesitated.

'Go on,' encouraged Thomas.

'I'm scared I'll have to be a lady and never have a farm at all,' said Millie in a rush. 'Grandpa, you couldn't leave the farm to me? Please?'

'I wish I could,' said Thomas gently. 'But your father and your grandfather have worked here all their lives. I couldn't take it away from them. I'll have a word with your father, though, I promise.'

I'll leave you money in my will too, he thought, to come to you at marriage or when you turn twenty-five. Enough to buy a farm and set it up, and if you've got it in you, you'll do well from there, even if your father leaves this place to others. But all he said out loud was: 'I have a present for you.'

Millie frowned. 'But it's your birthday, not mine.'

'Well, not really a present then. It's a cloak ... No, not a real cloak,' he added when the child looked around. 'It's a cloak in your mind. You imagine it, that's all. I've had it since I was your age.'

He'd thought Millie would look disappointed at that. But, instead she appeared interested.

'What do I do with it?'

'It's a courage cloak. I was your age when I found it. If you're scared you put it round your shoulders and ...' He paused.

'And you're not scared any more?' demanded Millie.

'Yes, you're still scared,' admitted Thomas. 'But you know that you can bear it. You know that being frightened will never stop you doing anything.'

The girl considered his words. Then she nodded. 'Is it mine now?'

'Yes,' said Thomas. 'It's yours. And when you've finished with it you can give it to your children in turn.'

The child nodded seriously. 'I'll take good care of it.'

Thomas watched her go, her small feet in their button boots, the flounces on her skirt, and sat back in his chair. People crossed the lawn in the last of the afternoon sunlight: women with lacy parasols; Joshua and James discussing sheep prices, most like; Marcus charming one of the Hazelton girls under a tree.

And, all at once, his vision blurred. He no longer saw the faces of his children, his grandchildren, the squatters and their wives, Captain Marcus Appleby — all carefully unconscious of their father's past.

Instead he saw the ghost again, gazing at him from the lawn. For the first time now he saw it clearly. It was a child, Millie's age perhaps, with dark hair and laughing eyes. Tom glanced hurriedly around, but no-one else had seen it. He looked back at the ghost, almost expecting it to have vanished again. But now there were other ghosts there, too, a host of children standing on the lawn, girls as well as boys. They smiled at him as though they knew what he had been, all that he had done, and their eyes were full of pride, and not embarrassment.

And suddenly Tom Appleby knew who his ghosts were.

They were his descendants. They were Millie's grandchildren, or her great-grandchildren maybe. They knew his past. And they no longer felt they had to hide their eyes from what their ancestor had been.

They were proud of him, these spirits of the future. They were curious about him, and they were proud.

Thomas Appleby raised his cane and saluted his spirits, then watched them fade slowly into the deepening shadows on the lawn. Would they care for what he left? He smiled. He'd have to trust them.

Thomas Appleby, chimney sweep and convict, grazier and magistrate, gazed out at his acres, and was content.

AUTHOR'S NOTES

The Story of the First Fleet and Settlement

One day, when I was four, my preschool teacher found me in the sandpit ladling sand from one bucket to another. She asked me what I was doing.

'I'm the quartermaster at Sydney Cove,' I said, 'giving out the rations to the convicts. If I give too much everyone will starve.'

My mother had told me bedtime stories of early Sydney when I was small: stories from the books she'd studied at university, bits from Watkin Tench's diary. She also told me stories from my great-something-grandmother's diary, written in those early years of the colony (the diary has been handed down from eldest daughter to eldest daughter for nearly 200 years).

So from a young age I knew that the story told in the history books at school wasn't absolutely true: the convicts transported for stealing a loaf of bread, the rotting ships of the First Fleet, the failed crops that caused people to starve.

Even when I was small I knew that one day I'd write a story of early Australia that didn't keep passing on these myths.

Crowded, rotting ships and dying convicts

By modern standards the journey of the First Fleet from England was hellish: crowded, stinking, poor food, stale water. By the standards of the day, however, it was a miracle voyage — in a nearly eight-month journey only three per cent of Captain Phillip's charges died (and those mostly from childbirth or illness they had when they came aboard), far fewer than would have died if they had stayed in prison in England, or even in the slums of London. There were no major outbreaks of disease once the ships left England.

Phillip went to extraordinary lengths to make sure that the ships were sound, that the convicts were fitted with good clothes and had as much fresh food as they could eat both before they left and at Rio and Cape Town — not the salted or dried food that was the staple for sea journeys at that time.

The land was barren, the crops failed

The land at Sydney Cove proved much less fertile than that on the Hawkesbury River or at Parramatta, and wheat especially didn't thrive there. But vegetable gardens grew abundantly, and so did maize and potatoes, vines and fruit trees. By September of the first year Captain Phillip wrote to Joseph Banks in England: 'Vegetables of all kinds are in plenty in my garden and I believe very few want them but from their own neglect'.

Captain Tench also recognised that, given manure, the soil of the colony would grow vegetables all year round. The early gardens gave their owners massive potatoes, giant cabbages, radish, turnips, beans, peas, tomatoes, endive, melons, cucumbers, pumpkins, strawberries, rhubarb, spinach ... (The people who underestimate how much vegetable food the early colony had obviously have never lived off their own vegetable garden!)

Fruit trees bore produce too, and grew so quickly that the settlers were stunned: in two years apples, oranges, figs, grapes, pomegranates and possibly others were bearing fruit.

Gardening freshly cleared ground, however, was much harder work than the colonists had expected. Though by 1790 nearly all the colonists, free or convict, had vegetable gardens, many merely scratched the soil and didn't bother carting water in dry times, or failed to add animal manure or even dig out tree roots.

The starving colony

This is another myth, though there is good reason for it. For many of the colonists believed they *were* starving. Certainly the first winter was difficult, and scurvy and dysentery were a problem, though the rations were fleshed out by the first vegetables grown in the colony, as well as wild spinach, berries, seaweeds, game and other food, though fish seemed scarce.

However, by the first summer vegetable gardens were providing abundantly, including such staples as maize and potatoes, and luxuries like melons, and there was wild food too.

Fish were plentiful in summer. There was meat from kangaroos, parrots, wallabies, emus, even though game was getting scarcer and powder for the muskets was in short supply. The colony ate crows, ducks, swans, and probably wild eggs and oysters as well.

In fact the colonists were arguably eating better than most of them ever had before — and were healthier too. The medical records show a steadily improving state of health, with improved fertility and lower death rate, very little scurvy — presumably only those who refused native fruits and wouldn't eat vegetables suffered — and no sign of deficiency diseases like pellagra.

How has the myth arisen?

To begin with, the colonists *were* hungry — hungry for the food they were familiar with, in particular meat and bread. Even when food was plentiful the marines and even the convicts grumbled about having to eat fish instead of pork and beef, or maize bread instead of wheat. Despite maize growing so much better than wheat in the first years of the colony, more land was planted to wheat, simply because they craved wheat flour.

'Real' food back in those days was bread and meat — preferably roasted. Vegetables were only eaten as a garnish for the meat, or fish for a first course. Only the poor ate lots of vegetables — and even the poor might have a blade of beef for Sunday dinner, and a pile of potatoes cooked in the baker's oven.

The diary of Thomas Turner (a not very well-off shopkeeper) at the time talked of suppers of roast mutton, with a cold veal pastie, some fried veal, a cold ham, tarts and so on — and this was just for an informal meeting with friends. Another day he ate a knuckle of veal and bacon, a beef pudding, and hard pudding and turnips — the only vegetables served in the entire meal!

By our standards the settlers at Sydney Cove expected to eat incredible amounts of varied meats three times a day, accompanied by ale or spirits, bread and tarts and puddings. Vegetables were simply not 'real food' at all.

There were real scarcities, though: by 1790 tools were scarce, and the colony had run out of candles, new clothes and many other necessities of a 'civilised life'. This added to the feelings of isolation, fear and terror that they had been cut off from the world — as indeed they had. It was depression and uncertainty that gripped the colony in these years more than genuine hunger.

There is another factor too. Our knowledge of those days comes from those able to read and write, those who wrote letters or diaries. They were the very ones who felt hungriest for their proper diet of meat and bread, and who found eating large amounts of vegetables so wearisome that often they went without. The marines' official dinners were foregone just for lack of meat, bread and spirits. Even Governor Phillip was trying to ensure that the colony received the supply ships they desperately needed — and not just for food. Nor could he be sure that the sporadic hunting and fishing efforts would continue to be successful. He had to paint as black a picture as possible in order to acquire what the colonists thought they needed.

The officers — most of whom didn't want to be in Australia in the first place — were not starving, though they may have thought they were. But they were depressed and isolated and, at times, afraid of what further scarcity might be to come.

Transported for stealing a handkerchief

Many convicts *were* transported for just such an offence — because if they had been convicted of the totality of their thefts they would have been hanged, and judges wanted to give them a chance in the colonies. So they were convicted on the smallest charge possible in order to escape the gallows. Most, however, were genuine criminals, given a chance of a new life in New South Wales. (Over half the convicts returned home when they had served their sentence, preferring slums and poverty to free land and hard work.)

No trained farmers

Governor Phillip had been a farmer in Hampshire; many of the marines had farming backgrounds, and some of the convicts had been farm labourers, if not farmers themselves.

Yes, many of the convicts didn't know one end of a hoe from the other; nor were they interested in tilling the land. Most convicts, like Tom, had been educated in the moral code of Newgate or the prison hulks on the Thames, where you took what you could and thought mostly of yourself or you didn't survive. They found it difficult to cooperate with each other, much less with the land.

But some skill was there and experience, too, for those who wished to take advantage of it. According to Governor Phillip in 1791, and other witnesses too, almost everyone in the colony had their own garden and many also had small orchards.

Another good — but exaggerated — tale is of the rapes and orgies on the first night the women came ashore, but that rests on the report of a man who wasn't even there, a surgeon on board ship. Captain Tench — who *was* there — just spoke of 'licentiousness' when the men and women came together. It was probably a fairly wild party, but not the horror it has been made out to be.

Or maybe it was. We are looking back more than 200 years, after all, trying to interpret evidence that still leaves much of the story untold. It is in those blank spaces that fiction can be written — as long as it doesn't contradict the records of those who were there.

Characters

The characters in this book are all imaginary, apart from historical figures like Captain Arthur Phillip,

Reverend Johnstone and Watkin Tench. Tom Appleby, Master Jack, Jem, Sam, Rob and the others, though, are composites of real people who did exist. Tom has large parts of John Hutton, the young chimney sweep who was transported to Australia, but he is based on one of my ancestors too.

The Sergeant's Cove doesn't exist though I based it on a real cove in Sydney Harbour. Other locations are real.

London language
The London streets had their own dialect, and chimney sweeps also had jargon of their own. I've used a few words of this to add flavour, but to make things clearer for the reader I've 'translated' the language into fairly modern speech.

'Indians'
This was the name most early colonists gave to the Aboriginal clans who lived around Port Jackson, who called themselves the Euroa, or 'the people'. Although several of the settlers tried to learn at least some of the local language, there was almost no understanding of local culture, in particular the Euroa's attempts to bring the newcomers into their traditions of gift exchange and social obligations.

Changing your story
When I was a child in the 1950s, my grandmother felt it was important to tell me that even though our family

had been here since the early settlement, none of her ancestors had *ever* been convicts.

Actually *most* of her ancestors who came to Australia had been convicts. All were well off by the end of their lives — and carefully hid their past.

For them, as for Tom in this book, Australia was a truly generous land.

JACKIE FRENCH

Jackie French's writing career spans 13 years, 39 wombats, 110 books for kids and adults, 15 languages, various awards, radio shows, newspaper and magazine columns, theories of pest and weed ecology and 28 shreddedback doormats. The doormats are the victims of the wombats, who require constant appeasement in the form of carrots, rolled oats and wombat nuts, which is one of the reasons for her prolific output: it pays the carrot bills.

Jackie's love of history began as a child and has been the inspiration for the series of books that began with *Somewhere Around the Corner*, *Daughter of the Regiment*, *Soldier on the Hill*, *Lady Dance*, *The White Ship* and *Valley of Gold*. Jackie feels that the past was not only a fascinating adventure, but also holds the clues to understanding our own time.

Jackie's most recent awards include the 2000 Children's Book Council Book of the Year Award for Younger Readers for the critically acclaimed, *Hitler's Daughter*, which also won the 2002 UK Wow! Award for the most inspiring children's book of the year; the 2002 Aurealis Award for Younger Readers for *Café on Callisto*; ACT Book of the Year for *In the Blood*; and for *Diary of a Wombat* with Bruce Whatley, the Children's Book Council Honour Book, NSW Koala Award for Best Picture Book, Nielsen Book Data / ABA Book of the Year Award, the Cuffie Award for favourite picture book (USA) and the American Literary Association (ALA) for notable children's book.

Visit Jackie's website **www.jackiefrench.com**
or
www.harpercollins.com.au/jackiefrench
for copies of her monthly newsletter

Non-fiction

Seasons of Content • How the Aliens From Alpha Centauri Invaded
My Maths Class and Turned Me into a Writer
How to Guzzle Your Garden • The Book of Challenges
Stamp, Stomp, Whomp (and other interesting ways to get rid of pests)
The Fascinating History of Your Lunch
Big Burps, Bare Bums and other Bad-Mannered Blunders
To the Moon and Back • Read it Right (September 2004)

Somewhere
around the
Corner

JACKIE FRENCH

Even in the depression you could dream of a better world

When Barbara becomes caught up in a wild demonstration, she is frightened and wants to escape. An old man she meets at the demonstration tells her to close her eyes, walk around the corner and arrive at a better place. The place she finds is 1934, the height of the Depression. Times are tough and  people are finding it hard to feed their families.

A boy called Young Jim comes to Barbara's aid and takes her on a journey to meet his family. They offer Barbara the love, security and peace that are missing from her own life. But their time isn't Barbara's time and she knows she may not be able to stay forever. Young Jim promises to look after Barbara always, but what will happen if she is forced to return to her own time? And does she have a choice?

Daughter
of the Regiment

JACKIE FRENCH

Harry and Cissie live 150 years apart.
What is the mystery that links them?

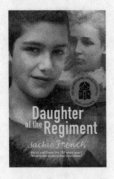

Cissie is an orphaned girl living with the soldiers at the garrison 150 years ago. Harry is about to leave his parents' farm to go to boarding school in the city. Harry can see Cissie through the floating hole in the chookhouse, but Cissie can't see him. Despite this they share a bond — a bond that Harry can't quite work out. All he knows is that something more powerful than time has drawn them together.

Soldier
on the Hill

JACKIE FRENCH

Can someone who saves your life be called an enemy?

The hole was moving! The walls were falling down ... There was a rope under his arms. There was a face above. An anxious face, yelling something down to him, something he didn't understand. A strange face, with something wrong about the eyes. Tanned skin, unshaven, black hair a bit too long ...

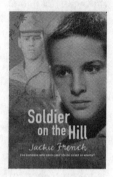

Joey knows there is a Japanese soldier hiding in the hills. It was a Japanese man, a soldier, who hauled him out of the mine shaft, who lit the fire to bring the searchers, and then disappeared. But nobody believes Joey.

Joey knows he will have to find the soldier himself. He must find him — he could be part of an invasion force sending secret messages to waiting submarines. Or could he?

It's World War Two and the world is in turmoil, but for Joey the enemy isn't as he imagined.

Hitler's Daughter

JACKIE FRENCH

A thought-provoking book about a story that could be true.
At least Mark is beginning to wonder if it is.

The bombs were falling, the smoke was rising from the concentration camps, but Hitler's daughter knew nothing of this. All she knew was the world of lessons with Fräulein Gelber, the hedgehogs she rescued from the cold and the exciting visits from her beloved father Duffi. Until the day she is taken to her father's bunker in Berlin ...

Anna's story about Hitler's daughter haunts Mark. Could it have been true? Did Hitler's daughter really exist? If Mark had a father like Hitler, could he love him?